Leslie pretende

She told herself her pr̶̶̶̶
long as neither Jeffrey̶̶̶̶
going on in her head, ̶̶̶̶
she knew she was fooling herself. The pretence
wasn't innocent. It was dangerous, because it wasn't
going to be real, and by continuing it and allowing
herself to revel in it, she was setting herself up to be
hurt in a big way.

But it didn't matter.

Nothing mattered except the knowledge that right
now there was nowhere else she'd rather be and no
one else she'd rather be with.

Dear Reader

As summer continues to sizzle, it is our pleasure to bring you this month's Special Edition™ line-up. In contrast to the weather that may be outside your window, two single parents are trapped in a blizzard in *Snow Baby* by Cathy Gillen Thacker. And there's another storm raging in *Stranded on the Ranch* by Pat Warren. Fortunately, there's something about being trapped indoors that seems to help love along…

Meanwhile, Laurie Paige is back this month with a tale of deliberate seduction. Jackson McLean knows Dawn Erickson is intended for his half-brother, but in revenge against the family that turned him away, he's determined to take her for himself. And in *The Cowboy Takes a Wife* there's another tale of family rifts. Zach Colby falls for a pregnant woman but the baby she's carrying is heir to an estate that's rightfully his!

Finally, Leslie Marlowe fulfils her dreams of marriage and motherhood in *A Mother for Jeffrey*. And don't miss *Partners in Marriage*, a heart-warming marriage of convenience story.

We hope you enjoy them all!

The Editors

A Mother for Jeffrey
TRISHA ALEXANDER

SILHOUETTE
SPECIAL EDITION®

This book is dedicated, with thanks and affection, to
Sandy Weider, who has never missed a book signing.
Sandy, you're the best!

*Silhouette, Silhouette Special Edition and Colophon are
registered trademarks of Harlequin Books S.A., used under licence.*

*First published in Great Britain 1999
Silhouette Books, Eton House, 18-24 Paradise Road,
Richmond, Surrey TW9 1SR*

© Patricia A. Kay 1998

ISBN 0 373 24211 5

23-9907

*Printed and bound in Spain
by Litografia Rosés S.A., Barcelona*

TRISHA ALEXANDER

always wanted to be a writer. Now that she is, she can't imagine ever doing anything else. When she's not creating stories, she loves to go to the movies, read other writers' books, see Broadway shows, play the organ and travel. Trisha and her husband of forty years live in Houston, Texas. They have three grown-up children and three wonderful grandchildren.

Other novels by Trisha Alexander

Silhouette Special Edition®

Cinderella Girl
When Somebody Loves You
When Somebody Needs You
Mother of the Groom
When Somebody Wants You
Here Comes the Groom
Say You Love Me
What Will the Children Think?
Let's Make It Legal
The Real Elizabeth Hollister...
The Girl Next Door

This Child Is Mine
*A Bride for Luke
*A Bride for John
*A Baby for Rebecca
Stop the Wedding!
Substitute Bride
With This Wedding Ring

Three Brides and a Baby

Chapter One

Brian Canfield left his office early Thursday afternoon. It was a beautiful, bright June day with a nice breeze coming in off the Gulf—just the kind of summer day Brian liked best. As he drove along Galveston's Seawall Boulevard, he sang along with the radio—an oldies Houston station that played his favorite sixties and seventies music.

The song ended, followed almost immediately by the Eagles' "Hotel California." Brian, in his slightly off-key voice, sang as much of the lyrics as he remembered.

Joy had always teased him about his voice. The thought brought a familiar ache to his heart. Actually, the ache was always there. The only difference was, some days it was buried deeper than other days.

The happiness he'd felt only moments earlier faded. It was fourteen months since Joy, his beloved wife, four months pregnant with their unborn child, had died in a freak accident while their little family was vacationing in London.

Fourteen hellish months, during which Brian had had to push aside his own feelings of anguish and loss to concentrate on his son, who had been sitting right next to Joy when the out-of-control car slammed into their table at a sidewalk café in Piccadilly Circus.

Brian had been so worried about Jeffrey. For months after the accident, he'd hardly spoken. Finally, in desperation, Brian had gotten his son into therapy, but for some reason, the first therapist had not been able to connect with Jeffrey. And then they'd been referred to Dr. Singer.

Thank God, under Dr. Singer's care, Jeffrey finally seemed to be recovering from the trauma of seeing his mother killed before his eyes. He still had bad days, of course. A child did not magically forget something as horrific as Jeffrey's experience, but at least now there were lots of good days, too.

Brian was still thinking about Jeffrey when, ten minutes later, he pulled his Suburban into the driveway of his home in one of Galveston's exclusive beach communities.

"Dad, hi!" Jeffrey, who was gluing together a model airplane on Brian's workbench in the garage, looked up from his labors and grinned.

Brian grinned back. "Hey, sport! That the new

model Gramps gave you?'' He walked into the garage and ruffled his son's sandy-colored hair, which was the exact shade of his own.

''Yeah. I've been workin' on it all afternoon. It's cool, isn't it?'' Jeffrey held up the nearly completed model of an F22 jet fighter plane. His hazel eyes, inherited from his mother, shone happily.

''It sure is. And you've done a great job with it.''

Jeffrey face shone with pleasure. ''Thanks.''

''Don't forget to clean everything up when you're done.''

''I won't.''

Brian walked up the three steps leading from the garage into the utility room, beyond which was the cheerful kitchen that, more than any other room in the house, bore the stamp of Joy's bubbling personality.

She had picked out the russet floor tiles, the bright wallpaper, the peach-colored countertops. She'd lovingly made the peach-striped tieback curtains and carefully scouted out the dark green cactus cookie jar and decorative bottles that dotted the counters.

She'd also chosen all the plants that adorned the windowsills and corners of the room. Since her death, Brian and his housekeeper had both attempted to keep them healthy-looking, but neither of them had Joy's green thumb, and some of the plants had already died.

Brian sighed. Nothing was the same without her, no matter how hard he tried to pretend it was. God, he missed her. In thousands of ways, he missed her.

Sometimes, the weight of his loneliness threatened to bury him, but he never let himself give way to it. He couldn't. He had Jeffrey to think of. If Brian allowed himself to succumb to self-pity, it would hurt Jeffrey. And Jeffrey had been hurt enough.

Pushing his bleak thoughts out of his mind, Brian walked over to the stove and lifted the lid of a pot that sat over a low flame. Chili simmered inside. Brian leaned over and sniffed. It smelled pretty good. Edie Hollis, the housekeeper he'd hired after Joy died, always fixed something for their supper before she left in the evenings. She wasn't a great cook, like Joy had been, but if her meals weren't imaginative, they were hearty, and she tried to make them balanced and healthy.

Just then, Edie, a sixty-something grandmother with clear blue eyes and a kind face, walked into the kitchen. She had a spray can of furniture polish and a dustcloth in her hands. "Well, hi, Mr. Canfield. You're home early tonight."

Brian had been trying to get Edie to call him Brian ever since her first day on the job, but she stubbornly persisted in addressing him as Mr. Canfield, saying it "wouldn't be seemly" to call him by his first name.

"Yes, the crew finished early." Brian owned a small construction company that specialized in commercial buildings. He was particularly pleased by this most recent project—a small shopping center that he'd managed to bring in two weeks ahead of its projected completion and without any cost overruns. He grinned at Edie. "So I'm celebrating, which means you can go home early tonight, too."

Her face lit up. "Oh, thank you! This'll help me so much, 'cause I have a pile of laundry to do before I leave tomorrow." But in the next instant, her brow furrowed. "You *did* remember that I'm leaving to go to my daughter's house in Ohio just as soon as I drop Jeffrey off at Dr. Singer's tomorrow?"

Brian nodded. Edie's daughter had given birth to a little boy ten days ago, and Edie had been chomping at the bit to see her new grandson. She would be gone a week. She'd worried about taking time off right now, because Joy's parents, who normally filled in when Brian needed backup child care, were in Canada for the summer, but Brian had assured Edie—more than once—that it was okay for her to be gone.

He had it all figured out. His next project—an elementary school—wasn't scheduled to start until the week after next, so the week Edie was gone would mainly be spent in the office. Brian figured he could bring Jeffrey in with him for part of each day, and the rest of the time, Brian would simply take off. That was the beauty of owning your own business. Although much of the time you worked longer hours and much harder than you would if you were working for someone else, you *did* have a certain freedom that made situations like this one easier to handle.

Since Joy's death, Brian had gained a new respect for single parents and the problems they faced, especially with child care and things like getting your kid to an appointment when you were supposed to be at work yourself.

He knew he was lucky. He could afford a good housekeeper, and he'd had Joy's parents to help him, too. Some people had no one. He couldn't imagine how they managed.

As Edie bustled about, putting the cleaning supplies away and gathering up her belongings, she gave Brian a steady stream of instructions.

"I made some spaghetti sauce and meatballs the other day, and they're in the freezer, in that container with the red lid. All you have to do is thaw it out, and of course, cook some spaghetti. I bought you that angel hair kind, 'cause it only takes three minutes to cook. You have to boil your water first, then put in the spaghetti. And don't forget to stir. The spaghetti will stick if you don't."

"I think I can handle it," Brian said in amusement.

"And there's also a meat loaf in the freezer. I wrapped it in aluminum foil, then put it in one of those freezer bags. I used one of those black markers to write on the top. *M-E-A-T L-O-A-F*. You can't miss it. You could just make some of those instant mashed potatoes to go with it. 'Course they won't be as good as homemade potatoes..." Her voice trailed off worriedly.

"Edie, quit worrying. Jeffrey and I will be fine. If nothing else, we could eat at Luby's every night." Luby's was a popular area cafeteria.

"Well, I just feel responsible. It's my job—"

"Will you get *out* of here?" Brian said, chuckling. "It's your job to go see that new grandson of yours. That's what's important right now."

Finally she left, via the garage, so she could "get one last hug from Jeffrey." Brian, who had skipped lunch, watched from the door. After she was gone, he said, "You hungry?" to Jeffrey.

"Kinda," Jeffrey said.

"Good. Supper will be ready in about five minutes."

"Okay."

"But clean up first."

"I *know,* Dad. You already *told* me."

Jeffrey's expression was long-suffering, and Brian grinned.

By the time Brian had set the table, taken the salad Edie had prepared out of the refrigerator, spooned out two bowls of chili, sliced some bread, and poured a glass of milk for Jeffrey, Jeffrey had walked inside.

"Go wash your hands," Brian said. He took the pitcher of iced tea from the refrigerator and poured himself a glass.

"Did you remember that I'll be picking you up from your appointment with Dr. Singer tomorrow?" Brian said, once they were settled at the table.

"Yeah, I remembered."

"I thought I might come early. Give me a chance to meet Leslie." Leslie Marlowe was Dr. Singer's office manager, and she and Jeffrey had become friends. Brian had never met the woman because the only time he'd ever been inside the office was for Jeffrey's first visit, and she had been on vacation that week.

Jeffrey's eyes brightened. "Cool."

Brian smothered a smile. The word "cool" was Jeffrey's favorite expression nowadays. Brian had heard the word so often, he had even started uttering it himself, which his secretary found hilarious.

For a while, they ate in silence.

About halfway through the meal, Jeffrey put his spoon down. "Dad..." he said hesitantly. "Do you ever think about Mom?"

The unexpected question felt like a punch in the gut, but Brian met his son's eyes steadily and answered without flinching. "Yes, son, I do."

"A lot?"

"Yes. A lot." Brian waited, sure there was more Jeffrey wanted to say. But when Jeffrey, head bowed so that Brian couldn't see his eyes, remained silent, Brian said gently, "You think about her a lot, too, don't you?"

Another long moment went by. Jeffrey finally looked up. His eyes were forlorn. "Yeah..." He swallowed. "But..."

"But what, son?"

"S-sometimes I—I can't remember her voice."

The admission tore at Brian's heart. "Jeffrey..." He reached across the table to touch his son's forearm. "It's okay, you know."

"But how could I forget how she sounded, Dad?"

It was at times like these that Brian felt most helpless. His son needed him now. Needed him to be strong and wise. Needed him to say something comforting. Something that would make the guilt disappear. Brian chose his words carefully. "It really is okay." He squeezed Jeffrey's arm. "Sometimes I forget how her voice sounded, too."

"You *do?*"

Brian nodded. "It's normal."

"It *is?*"

"Yes. It happens to everyone. Haven't you talked to Dr. Singer about this?"

Jeffrey shook his head.

"Why not? I thought you talked to him about everything."

"I do, but, it's just..." Jeffrey's voice trailed off.

"Just what?"

Jeffrey shrugged. "I don't know. It...it seemed wrong."

"Wrong to talk to him?"

"No. Wrong to forget."

For a moment, Brian couldn't think what to say, and then, from somewhere, he pulled the right words. "Son, just because sometimes you can't remember doesn't mean you don't still love Mom."

Jeffrey ducked his head again. And Brian knew if he could see his son's eyes, they'd be filled with tears.

Brian fought his own urge to cry. When he spoke, his voice was rough with emotion. "And Mom loves you, too. Right now, I'll bet she's looking down from Heaven and telling you not to feel bad.''

Jeffrey nodded. Then, a few moments later, he sighed and began to eat again.

That night, as Brian lay in his solitary bed, he kept thinking about the conversation and how much Jeffrey had had to deal with since losing his mother.

Thankfully, he had seemed to accept Brian's explanation about the normality of sometimes not being able to recall what Joy sounded like. Brian wished it were as simple to banish the guilt he felt.

If he lived to be a hundred, he would never forget that day. They had prepared for their trip to London with such happiness and excitement. Jeffrey, who was in the third grade at the time, was having his spring break that week, and on the spur of the moment, Brian and Joy had decided to take advantage of an airline promotion offering half-price round-trip fares.

"Why not?" Brian had said, even though he was not usually the spontaneous one in their marriage. "We have something terrific to celebrate, so let's do it in style."

Six weeks earlier, Joy had found out she was pregnant again, and they were still both floating on air over the news. They had been married twelve years and had finally become resigned to the disappointing fact that nine-year-old Jeffrey would probably be an only child.

And so they'd gone to London for their impromptu vacation. They'd been there four days. Four wonderful days into which they'd crammed all the sight-seeing they could. That particular afternoon had been unusually mild and sunny for London, and after several hours of walking, Joy had laughingly said, "Listen, you two. You may be able to walk forever, but I'm tired. Us moms-to-be need to rest our weary feet once in a while." She pointed down the block. "Let's stop at that café and get something to drink, okay?"

Brian finished his drink faster than Joy or Jeffrey and, spying a camera shop across the street, said, "While you two finish up, I'm going to go over there and buy some more film. I'm almost out."

Joy gave him an indulgent smile and refrained from pointing out that he'd already shot at least half a dozen rolls of film.

So Brian went to the camera shop, got his film, and was standing at the counter paying the clerk when the accident happened. He wasn't even looking. His first awareness of the tragedy was the sound of the impact, followed immediately by the screams of onlookers.

It took a moment or two for awareness to hit. And when it did, he raced across the street, fighting his way through the crowd, all the while shouting Joy's and Jeffrey's names. When he finally saw what was left of the table where they had been sitting, he'd thought they were both dead.

After that, everything was a blur. He barely remembered the days that followed. The only reason he was able to function at all was the knowledge that he couldn't fall apart because his son needed him.

Jeffrey still needed him.

And Brian would never let him down. As he had hundreds of times since Joy's death, he silently vowed he would devote the rest of his life to making sure nothing ever hurt Jeffrey again.

In Sunday school, Jeffrey had learned about Heaven. He wondered if it was true that when you died, you went to this beautiful place up in the clouds where God watched over you, and everyone was happy and nothing bad ever happened. Dad seemed to think it was.

He tried to picture his mother there. She had loved to sing and play the piano. What if there weren't any pianos in Heaven? How could she be happy without a piano?

When he was little, he thought only old people died. Older than his mom, anyhow. But then one of the kids in his third-grade class had died from some kind of cancer, and now Jeffrey understood that anyone could die.

It didn't seem fair, though. Some people lived to be real old. On TV once he'd seen this man, he was a hundred years old. Jeffrey's mom had only been thirty-four when she died. Why was it some people got to live to be one hundred and others died when they were nine, like Jeffrey's friend from third grade? That sure wasn't fair.

That's why lately Jeffrey had been wondering if

there really *was* a God, because if there was, wouldn't He have planned things better? Why would God take away somebody's mother or somebody's kid?

Every time he thought stuff like that, he felt guilty. If his dad or his grandparents knew he was having these thoughts, they'd be upset. In Sunday school, he'd been taught that you were supposed to have faith. When he was little, he hadn't understood what faith meant. Now he knew it meant believing whatever you were told.

The trouble was, his mother had told him she'd always be there for him, and that had turned out not to be true. What if all this stuff about faith and Heaven wasn't true either?

That night, as he got ready for bed, he decided that if his mother was *really* up in Heaven and there *really* was a God, and God was *really* all-powerful, like Superman or something, then He ought to be able to let his Mom send Jeffrey some answers. So after his father had tucked him in, said good-night and left the room, Jeffrey got out of bed and knelt by the window. He looked up at the sky where Heaven supposedly was.

"Dear Mom," he prayed, "I hope you can hear me. I've been thinkin' about you a lot lately, and I really need to know if you're okay and you're happy now. Because if you are and you could somehow let me know, then I could tell Dad, and maybe then he and I could be happy again, too."

When he was finished, he felt better, almost like his mother had *already* answered him.

The alarm buzzed at six Friday morning, just the way it did every weekday. Leslie Marlowe automatically reached over and turned it off. She knew she should get up, but she decided it wouldn't hurt if she just stayed where she was for another few minutes.

Forty-five minutes later, her eyes popped open. She didn't even have to look at the bedside clock to know she'd overslept. Sure enough, it was now six forty-five, and that meant she was going to have to move very fast if she hoped to make it to work on time.

The answering service had already taken half a dozen calls by the time Leslie arrived at the office and checked with them. She wrote down the messages, knowing she should return the calls immediately, but five or ten more minutes wasn't going to make that much of a difference, so instead she headed for the small kitchenette where she started the coffeemaker.

She'd stopped at the doughnut shop on the way in and picked up two crullers, the same way she had every morning for the past eleven years. If she hadn't, Dr. Singer would have had her head on a plate. He'd made it very clear that he expected his doughnuts, and that it was her job to make sure they were there.

She smiled, thinking of her boss and his sweet

tooth. Dr. Singer was a real softy, just like the crullers he so loved. Leslie had worked for him ever since her divorce. She still felt grateful to him for taking a chance on a completely inexperienced twenty-four-year-old woman who had never held a paying job. Consequently, she never resented doing anything he asked her to do—even if the task didn't fall strictly into her capacity as office manager. She had always considered the personal errands she carried out for him to be her contribution to making her boss's life run more smoothly so that he could devote his energies to improving the quality of life for his young patients.

Once, after she'd been working for him for a few months, she'd asked him why he'd hired her when there had probably been dozens of more qualified people. He didn't hesitate. "Because I like red hair," he said. His eyes twinkled. "That's why I have an Irish setter at home and a pretty redhead in the office."

Leslie had laughed then, and she laughed now, remembering. Despite his teasing, it hadn't taken her very long to realize the real reason Dr. Singer had hired her was his affinity for hopeless cases. And Leslie had definitely been a hopeless case. Inexperienced, devastated by her divorce, riddled with self-doubt after five years of Elliott's putdowns, and scared to death she couldn't make it on her own and might have to go back to her parents' home.

But somehow she'd pulled herself together enough to begin looking for a job within days of

Elliott's moving out. She'd answered Dr. Singer's ad the first week. And three weeks later, she had her first paycheck. She would never forget how giddy she'd felt as she'd held it in her hands. The first money she'd ever earned!

As she reminisced, she prepared for the day. Dr. Singer had a full schedule of patients beginning at nine o'clock, which was now less than thirty minutes away. Finishing in the kitchen, she walked back out to her office and looked at the appointment book.

That done, she picked up the message slips and headed for the small room adjoining Dr. Singer's office where she pulled the first few files he would need this morning.

Just as she finished, she heard Dr. Singer unlocking the back door. "Good morning," she said as she walked down the hall to meet him.

He smiled. "Morning, Leslie. Coffee ready?"

"Yes, it is, and your doughnuts are waiting for you, as well."

"Good." He removed his dark blue suit jacket and hung it in the hall closet, then preceded her into the kitchenette. After he'd poured a mug of coffee and helped himself to a doughnut, she poured herself a cup and stood watching him. He was a nice-looking man in his early sixties, with thick gray hair and matching gray eyes behind wire rimmed trifocals. He had a ruddy complexion, as if he spent a lot of time outdoors, but Leslie knew he didn't. His work was his life, and his leisure time was spent reading biographies and history, or playing chess with one of his longtime cronies.

"Any messages?" he asked around a mouthful of cruller.

Leslie handed him the message slips.

He looked through them swiftly. "Mrs. Rasley can wait. So can Mr. McKee and Dr. Luther. But I think I'd better give Elizabeth Wilkinson's mother a call before I see the first patient."

Leslie nodded.

Dr. Singer proceeded to rattle off several more instructions, and when he was finished, he headed toward his office and Leslie, carrying her cup of coffee, went back to the front desk.

She sat down and turned on her computer.

The day had officially started.

Six hours later, the bell announcing someone's arrival tinkled softly. Leslie looked up from her computer.

"Hi, Leslie."

She smiled at the sandy-haired youngster who had just walked through the office door. He was her favorite of all Dr. Singer's patients, exactly the kind of son she'd have loved to have herself.

"Well, hi, Jeffrey, you're early today."

Jeffrey Canfield's hazel eyes shone brightly, a decided improvement from the dullness that had filled them the first time Leslie had met the boy. "Yeah." He walked over to her desk. "Edie's going to Ohio, and she hadda drop me off early."

"Oh, that's right. She has a new grandson, doesn't she?" Leslie knew from previous conversations that Edie Hollis was the housekeeper Jeffrey's father had hired when his mother had died.

"Uh-huh."

"So what will you do all next week while she's gone? Go to your grandparents' house?"

He shook his head. "I can't. My grandparents are in Canada. They go there in the summertime."

"You're not going to stay by yourself, are you?" Although Jeffrey had recently turned eleven, Leslie felt he was too young to be home alone.

"Nope. My Dad's gonna let me go in to work with him or else he'll be home. We have a lot of things planned."

"That's good." She smiled at the boy, thinking what a sweetheart he was.

"Even though you're early, I'm afraid Dr. Singer won't be able to see you until four." Leslie gestured to the closed door of the inner office.

Jeffrey shrugged. "That's okay."

"Do you want to watch television?" After years of resisting, Leslie's boss had finally relented and put a small television set in his waiting area.

"Sure. But first…I—I have something for you."

"You do?"

He nodded, reaching into his jeans pocket and withdrawing a large, pale coral seashell.

"Oh, Jeffrey, it's *beautiful*," Leslie said, accepting the shell. She was enormously touched that he had remembered her once mentioning she collected seashells. "I love it. Thank you."

He ducked his head shyly. "You don't have one like it, do you?"

"No, I don't. It's simply wonderful. It's going to occupy a place of honor in my collection. In fact, I might not even take it home. I might just put it right here, on my desk, where I can look at it every day." So saying, she placed it next to a small crystal vase containing silk flowers.

The pleased smile that lit up his face tugged at Leslie's heart. Not for the first time, she wondered what his mother had been like. And what his father was like now. They had to be nice people to have produced such a thoughtful child.

"Now let's see what I can find for you to watch on TV." Leslie picked up the remote and hit the numbers for the Disney Channel. A movie about a boy and girl in Alaska was showing. "This okay?"

"Yeah, this is cool." Jeffrey walked over and plopped down Indian fashion in front of the TV.

"Not so close," Leslie cautioned. Realizing she sounded just like a mother, she smiled wistfully. Even though it had been almost twelve years since her last—and fourth—miscarriage, she had never been able to completely banish the feelings of sadness and deep regret that she would never experience motherhood.

Lately, and especially on days like this, when a child she would have given anything to call her own crossed her path, she had been thinking about adoption. She knew it was still difficult for a single woman or man to adopt, but it wasn't impossible.

Do it, something inside her urged. *At least look into it. After all, what have you got to lose? And look at what you stand to gain.*

Even as she tried to convince herself to proceed with at least an inquiry, she knew she was lying to herself. It wasn't true she had nothing to lose. At least now, she still had hope. But if she were turned down for an adoption, even that would be gone.

Could she live without hope?

Lots of women did.

Lots of women were childless, many of them not by choice. And they managed to build good lives. Meaningful lives. Productive lives.

You're a strong woman, Leslie. A survivor. You can handle anything.

The words of her former therapist, words Leslie now lived by, thrummed through her mind.

Looking again at Jeffrey, who was now absorbed by the tale unfolding on the TV screen, she squared her shoulders.

She would do it.

In fact, she would begin next week by investigating some agencies.

Excitement crowded out the sadness and regret she'd felt only moments earlier. Who knew? Maybe by this time next year, she would have a child of her own to love and care for, and she could finally stop pining after other people's.

Chapter Two

"Don't forget you're supposed to pick up Jeffrey in an hour."

Brian looked up from the plans for a six-story office building that were spread across his desk. Brenda Donatelli, his longtime secretary and good friend, stood in the open doorway of his office.

"I hadn't forgotten. As a matter of fact..." He stood and stretched. "I think I'll quit for the day and drive over there now."

"If you leave now, you'll be way too early," she warned. "And you know how you hate waiting."

Sometimes Brian wanted to tell her to stop mothering him, but he knew she meant well, and that she worried about him, especially since Joy's death. He also knew he was about the same age as Brenda's son, so she probably couldn't help herself. "I'm going early on purpose." If he didn't explain, she would simply question him until he did, so he added, "I want to meet Dr. Singer's office manager. You know, the woman Jeffrey's so high on."

"Good idea," Brenda enthused. "I've been real curious about her myself."

Brian smothered a smile. Brenda was "real curious" about everything. Some might even classify her curiosity as plain nosiness. But her nosiness had come in handy more than once, because she knew everything that was going on with their employees and kept Brian informed of anything he needed to know. "In that case," he said dryly, "I'll be sure and check her out thoroughly so I can give you a full report on Monday."

She grinned, not the least offended. After she'd walked back into her own office, Brian rolled up the plans and tucked them into their cubicle, turned off his computer, locked his desk and filing cabinet, and picked up his briefcase.

"Why don't you pack it up and go home now, too?" he said as he passed Brenda's desk.

"But I have so much to do."

"It'll still be here next week. And it isn't often we have a breather like this." In fact, for the past year, Brian couldn't remember another time when they'd had any break at all between jobs. And many times, jobs had overlapped, causing them all kinds of problems, because Brian only had two crews, and that was the way he wanted to keep it. "So you go on."

Her dark eyes shone happily. "Well, if you really mean it…"

"I mean it."

"Then I'm outta here. Tiffany wanted me to take her to a movie tonight, so now we can get an early start." Tiffany was Brenda's nine-year-old granddaughter, whom she was raising since the death of her daughter and son-in-law in a boating accident five years earlier.

They said their goodbyes and Brian left. As he drove toward Galveston's medical center, he finally admitted to himself that he was every bit as curious about Leslie Marlowe as Brenda was. When Jeffrey had first mentioned Dr. Singer's office manager, Brian got the idea she was a motherly, older woman—kind of like Brenda—and when he'd said as much to Jeffrey, Jeffrey had answered, in typical kid fashion, "Yeah, she's pretty old. You know. Like you, Dad."

Brian grinned again, remembering. There was a time when thirty-eight had seemed old to him, too. Actually, he remembered when *thirty* had seemed old, so this Leslie might actually be a fairly young woman. Well, he'd soon see.

It only took Brian ten minutes to reach the complex housing the medical center. Dr. Singer's office was located in an office building directly across the street. Brian parked the Suburban in the parking lot at the rear of the building, then headed for the fourth floor.

As he walked through the double glass doors of the psychologist's office, the woman sitting at the big L-shaped walnut desk in the middle of the reception area looked up, a welcoming smile on her face.

Brian took one look at Leslie Marlowe's warm brown eyes, auburn hair, and friendly face and immediately understood his son's attraction to the woman. Although other than the color of her hair, which was almost identical to Joy's, there was really no physical resemblance between the two women, there was something about Leslie Marlowe's face and, in particular, her smile, that reminded him strongly of his wife. For a moment, he was so unnerved by this discovery that he just stood there.

"May I help you?" she said.

Brian gave himself a mental shake and walked forward. "I'm Brian Canfield, Jeffrey's father."

"Oh! Hello." She stood then, and Brian saw that she was tall—much taller than she'd looked sitting down. Brian was just over six feet himself, and he didn't have to look down very far to meet Leslie Marlowe's eyes. Her height was a major difference between her and Joy, who had been a petite five foot three.

Leslie extended her hand. "I'm so glad to finally meet you," she said as they shook hands. "Jeffrey talks about you all the time."

Brian nodded. "He talks about you all the time,

too." *And now I know why.* His mind whirled. Jeffrey might not be consciously aware of the similarities between this woman and his mother, but Brian was suddenly sure—*uneasily* sure—that those similarities had everything to do with his son's feelings for Leslie.

Her smile had widened in pleasure. "He does?"

"Yes, he does." Remembering what he'd intended to tell her, he added, "In fact, that's why I came early today. I wanted a chance to meet you and thank you for being so nice to Jeffrey."

"You don't have to thank me. It's easy to be nice to Jeffrey. He's a great kid."

Brian shrugged. "I think he is, but I'm prejudiced."

"Well, I'm not. I'm around children all day long. And Jeffrey is special." She picked up a seashell from her desk. "Today he brought me this, because once I mentioned to him that I collect shells. How many eleven-year-old boys would think to do something like that?"

Her disclosure only added to Brian's disquiet, because Jeffrey hadn't mentioned anything about the seashell, and normally, he told Brian everything.

And she was right. The gift was not the kind of gesture a young boy would normally make. In fact, Brian couldn't remember Jeffrey *ever* doing anything like that on his own. Usually Brian had to remind him of his grandmother's birthday or some other special occasion where he needed to give a gift.

As if she sensed his concern, Leslie frowned slightly, and Brian made a concerted effort to wipe his mind free of his disturbing thoughts. Time enough to think about her and the impact she'd made on Jeffrey when Brian was alone. But he couldn't help feeling that Jeffrey's interest in and attachment to Leslie Marlowe couldn't be a healthy one. Because no matter what Jeffrey might be subconsciously wishing, Leslie Marlowe was not his mother.

Brian Canfield was silent for so long, Leslie wondered if she'd said something she shouldn't have. Was Jeffrey's father upset that Jeffrey had given her the seashell?

But why would he be? It wasn't as if Jeffrey had spent money on the gift. And, as far as she knew, Jeffrey's mother hadn't collected seashells or anything, because surely Jeffrey would have said so when Leslie had first mentioned her collection.

Bewildered, she searched Brian's face for a hint as to his thoughts, but there was no clue in his closed expression. Maybe he just didn't like her. It bothered her to think that might be the case.

"Jeffrey's going to be a while," she said to fill the awkward gap. "So why don't you have a seat? There are some magazines, or I could turn on the TV. Would you like some coffee or a soft drink while you wait?"

You're babbling, Leslie. Settle down. So what if he doesn't like you? Not everyone has to like you.

He shook his head. "Thanks, I'm fine." He walked over to one of the plaid armchairs grouped around a magazine-laden coffee table and sat.

Leslie sat down again, too. As he leafed through the magazines, she covertly studied him. He was a nice-looking man, although not classically handsome. His nose was too big and his jaw too square, but he had a rugged, solid look about him that was enormously appealing. His short hair was thick and straight, the same sandy color as his son's, and his eyes were a deep, dark blue. He had the tanned, sunweathered skin of a person who spent lots of time outdoors. Leslie remembered from Jeffrey's file that Brian owned a construction company. Yes, she could see him in a hard hat, working alongside his men.

Once more she wondered what she might have said or done to make Brian Canfield take a dislike to her. And he must have. Because he hadn't even smiled at her when he'd met her. In fact, he hadn't smiled at all since walking into the office.

Just then, he looked up, and Leslie, flustered to be caught staring at him, hurriedly pretended to be searching for something on her desk. She extracted a file from the pile in front of her and turned back to her computer. For the next ten minutes, she forced herself to work and not look at Brian Canfield, but she was acutely aware of him behind her.

"Um, Miss Marlowe?"

She turned and their eyes met.

"On second thought, I think I'll take you up on the coffee."

"Okay." She got up. "On one condition. No more of this Miss Marlowe stuff. The name is Leslie." For a moment, she was sure she'd made a mistake in trying to force him into a friendliness he didn't feel.

And then, slowly, a grin spread across his face. "Leslie it is. But only if you call me Brian."

Now she felt silly. He didn't dislike her. He was probably just reserved. Or maybe even shy. She returned his smile. "It's a deal. How do you take your coffee?"

"Black, one sugar."

"Coming right up."

Back in the kitchenette, she lectured herself not to make snap judgments about people. She certainly should know better. If working for Dr. Singer had taught her anything it was that the reasons behind a person's behavior were often quite different from what we perceived them to be. The trouble with most people, herself included, was that they tended to internalize everything. Most times, the way other people acted had nothing to do with you. If a sales clerk was cranky, it might be because she had cramps or her boyfriend had dumped her.

This time, when Leslie returned to the reception area and her desk, she didn't pretend to resume her work. She waited until Brian had drunk some of his coffee, then said, "So, are you pleased with Jeffrey's progress?"

He nodded. "Very much so."

"Dr. Singer is a wonderful doctor."

Brian drank some more of his coffee. "How long have you worked for him?"

"Eleven years."

"That's a long time."

"I know, but it doesn't seem like it. The time has really gone fast."

"You like your job, don't you?"

"I love my job."

He smiled again. "That's why the time has gone fast."

He should definitely smile more often. Leslie felt that if a man's eyes revealed his soul, his smile revealed his heart. Too bad she hadn't understood that when she'd met Elliott, she thought with just a trace of bitterness.

Just then, the inner door opened and Jeffrey emerged. His eyes brightened when he saw his father. "Dad! Hi! I didn't know you were here already."

Brian stood, putting an arm around Jeffrey's shoulders and giving him a look of such love and pride, it almost hurt Leslie to see it. A pang of loneliness stung her.

"Hey, sport," he said. "You ready to go?"

"Uh-huh."

Brian looked at her. "I guess we'll be on our way, then. Nice meeting you, Leslie."

"It was nice meeting you, too."

"Dad?" Jeffrey said. "Are we going for pizza now?"

"Don't we always go for pizza on Friday night?" Brian countered.

Leslie's yearning for a child, her yearning to be part of a loving family unit, yearnings she normally buried successfully, welled up for the second time that day. Wouldn't it be wonderful to have a son like Jeffrey? Someone to take to movies and out for pizza? Someone upon whom she could pour all her stored-up mother love?

"Do you like pizza, Leslie?" Jeffrey said, looking at her.

She forced herself to smile casually. "Who doesn't love pizza?"

"Dad, can Leslie go with us?" Jeffrey said eagerly.

Although it was only there an instant, Leslie saw the frown pass over Brian's face before he answered. "Well, sure, if she wants—"

"Oh, no, I couldn't go," Leslie interjected quickly. Her face felt warm with embarrassment. Did Jeffrey's father think she had been angling for an invitation when she'd said she loved pizza?

"Why not?" Jeffrey said. "You're gettin' ready to go home now, aren't you?"

Leslie *was* getting ready to go home. Jeffrey was the last appointment for the day, and he knew it, so there was no sense lying. "Yes, but I have some errands to run."

"You don't *have* to do 'em now, do you?" Jeffrey said. "Can't you do 'em later?" Not waiting for her to answer, he turned to his father again. "Please, Dad, can't Leslie come with us?"

"Son, I don't think she wants to."

"Sure she does," Jeffrey said happily. "Don't you want to, Leslie?"

"Well, I..." She stopped, not knowing what to say, torn between not embarrassing Brian and not hurting Jeffrey's feelings.

"See, Dad?" Jeffrey said. "She wants to come."

Brian smiled warmly as he met her eyes. "It would give both of us great pleasure if you would come with us."

Leslie told herself that if he'd issued the invitation grudgingly, she would have immediately and firmly refused. But Brian certainly seemed sincere. He'd probably frowned initially because he was taken aback by Jeffrey's suggestion. And she suddenly wanted to go, very much. She told herself the reason was because she wanted to know more about Jeffrey's father, but down deep, she knew that wasn't the only reason.

"Well, in that case...sure, I'd love to go with you." She ignored the little voice inside that said Brian could hardly have done otherwise than pretend to want her with them, when Jeffrey so obviously did. And when Brian so obviously would do anything for his adored son.

Jeffrey grinned. "Do you wanna ride in our car? Can she ride with us, Dad?"

"Sure."

"No, no, that's okay. I have to clean off my desk and talk to Dr. Singer for a few minutes before I leave," Leslie said. "I'll just meet you there. Where are you planning to go?"

"We're going to Pizza Heaven on 51st Street," Brian said. "It's just south of Broadway."

"I know exactly where it is," Leslie said. Although she'd never been there, she'd passed it many times.

The minute the door closed behind them, doubts assailed her about the wisdom of joining them. She shouldn't have said she'd go. Brian didn't want her with them. Why would he? He barely knew her. Jeffrey simply hadn't given him any choice.

She bit her lip. Well, it was too late to change her mind. They were gone, and if she didn't show up, Jeffrey would be upset and worried, and Brian would think she was nuts. Okay, so she would join them, but she wouldn't stay long. "I'll just eat a couple of pieces of pizza, then I'll make some kind of excuse, and I'll leave," she mumbled.

"Talking to yourself again, I see."

Leslie jumped. She hadn't heard Dr. Singer walk up behind her.

He was smiling at her. "You going home?"

Embarrassed, she felt her face coloring. Now Dr. Singer would think she was nuts. And he wouldn't be far wrong. She thought about telling him she was meeting Brian and Jeffrey for pizza, but for some reason, she felt awkward about it. "Yes, I—I was planning to. Unless you need something else?"

"No, no, you go on. Have a nice weekend, and I'll see you Monday."

For a moment, she felt guilty, as if she were doing something wrong by not having mentioned joining the Canfields at the pizza parlor. Then she told herself she was being silly again. "See you Monday," she echoed.

It took Leslie a bit longer to get to Pizza Heaven than it normally would have, because traffic was always heavy on Friday afternoons, both coming to the island and leaving it—and the renovations to the causeway bridge, which supposedly were on the drawing board, hadn't even begun. She could just imagine what rush hour would be like then. Thank goodness she both lived and worked on the main part of the island and really didn't have to battle traffic much.

So it was a good fifteen minutes after leaving the office before she pulled her five-year-old Toyota into the gravel parking lot behind the popular pizza place. Tempting aromas of yeast and peppers and tomato sauce greeted her as she walked inside.

She looked around, finally spotting Brian and Jeffrey, who were seated in a booth on the right side of the noisy room. Typical of most places that catered to kids, Pizza Heaven sported a video arcade containing a dozen machines being played by youngsters of all ages and a cacophony of bells and whistles and sirenlike wails filled the air.

"We waited to order until you got here," Jeffrey

said. He and his father were seated on opposite sides of the booth, so Leslie slid in next to Jeffrey.

"Jeffrey votes for pepperoni, but I'm open," Brian said.

"I like anything, as long as it doesn't have pepperoni or sausage," Leslie said. She wished she didn't feel like an interloper.

"Are you a vegetarian?" Brian asked.

"Not really. I just don't like fatty meats."

"I probably shouldn't." Brian's smile turned rueful. "My cholesterol is on the high side. But I can't give up an occasional sausage sandwich or big, thick, juicy steak."

"Well, it doesn't hurt anyone to indulge occasionally," Leslie said. "The key to anything is moderation, don't you think?"

"I agree. It's my doctor who needs convincing. I wish you'd call and talk to him for me." He grinned.

"I'm hungry, Dad," Jeffrey said.

"That's a not-so-subtle hint to quit talking and order," Brian said, laughing.

Leslie smiled. He was being awfully nice. Maybe he really didn't mind that she'd joined them.

They decided on a small pepperoni pizza for Jeffrey and a large mushroom–black olive–green pepper one for them. A few minutes later, their waiter brought their drinks and Brian placed their order.

When the waiter left, Brian said, "Sorry about the noise in here."

"It doesn't bother me," Leslie answered. In contrast to her house, which was far too quiet most of the time, she loved the noise kids made.

Almost as if he'd read her mind, Brian said, "Where do you live, Leslie?"

"I have a house near the Strand. On Sealy."

"Really?"

She smiled. "I know. People are always surprised to find out I live in the historic district. I inherited the house," she explained. "It's been in my mother's family for more than a hundred and fifty years." And it was a very sore point with her mother that the house had been left to Leslie by her grand-mother and not to Peggy.

"Wow," he said.

"She paints houses, Dad," Jeffrey said.

Leslie laughed at the look on Brian's face. "Not literally. I do watercolors of the historic homes in the area."

"For a minute there, I was thinking of hiring you to work for me. It's hard to find good painters."

"Oh, that's right, you're in construction. Do you build houses?"

"I have, in the past. Now we concentrate on com-mercial building."

They continued to talk casually as they waited for their pizza and then while they ate. Jeffrey, after eating three pieces, said, "Can I go play video games now, Dad?"

"Sure." Brian dug in his pocket and fished out some change.

Once Jeffrey was gone, there were a few moments

of awkward silence between them, then they both spoke at once.

"What do—"

"Do you—"

They both broke off and laughed.

"You go first," Brian said.

"No, you," Leslie said.

"I insist."

"Okay." She sat back. "Do you and Jeffrey plan to take a vacation this summer?"

A cloud passed over his face, and Leslie immediately realized her mistake. It had been while they'd been on vacation that his wife had been killed. She mentally kicked herself. How could she have forgotten?

"We haven't made any plans," he said. "What about you?"

"I don't normally go anywhere during the summer. But in the fall my best friend and I usually go to New York."

"I've never been to New York."

"I love the city," Leslie said, wishing the sadness in his eyes would disappear. "The museums, the galleries, the shows. It's wonderful." *Why did I have to remind him of the accident?*

"That's right, you're an artist. Tell me about your painting."

Leslie shrugged. "Not much to tell. I started painting as therapy when I was going through a bad time personally. At first it was just a way to lose myself. But very soon I realized I loved it. Now it's kind of an obsession.''

"But a nice obsession.''

"Yes, I think so.''

"Are you good at it?''

She smiled. "I'm getting better all the time.''

"You didn't answer my question.''

"I'm not the kind of person to toot my own horn.''

"Okay, I'll put it this way. Have you sold any of your paintings?''

"A few.''

"Then you must be good.''

Determined to keep the conversation light from now on, Leslie said, "What do *you* do for pleasure?''

He shrugged. "I used to golf, but now I spend most of my free time with Jeffrey.''

Leslie thought how if she had a son like Jeffrey, she would do the same thing.

"You probably think I'm overprotective,'' he said.

"I was thinking no such thing.''

"It's just that since his mother died, I don't like to leave him alone unless I have to.''

"Under the circumstances, that's perfectly natural.''

"Is it? Sometimes I worry that he isn't leading a normal enough kind of life.'' Looking over her shoulder, he smiled. "Here he comes now.''

"Can I have some more money, Dad?" Jeffrey said, walking up to their booth.

"I think you've had enough." Brian looked at his watch.

It was only then that Leslie realized she had stayed much longer than she'd intended. Picking up her purse, she said, "I didn't realize how late it is. If I'm going to get my errands run before the shops close, I'd better get going." She slid out of the booth. "Thank you for inviting me. I had a very nice time."

Brian stood, too. "We enjoyed having you."

"Bye, Jeffrey," Leslie said. "See you next week."

"Bye, Leslie."

She turned back to Brian. "Goodbye, Brian. Thanks again."

A small part of her hoped he would say something about doing it again, but the sensible part of her knew that wasn't going to happen. The only reason she was there with them now was because of Jeffrey.

Brian Canfield was not interested in her.

Brian Canfield was not interested in any woman. He was still mourning the death of his wife. That had been obvious earlier when she'd stuck her foot in her mouth and mentioned the vacation.

Later, as Leslie ran her errands, she told herself it was for the best that he'd not suggested seeing her again. Brian Canfield came with too much emotional baggage.

And additional emotional baggage was the last thing she needed in her life.

Chapter Three

"Leslie's nice, isn't she?"

"Yes, she is," Brian agreed. They were on their way home.

Brian hadn't really wanted Leslie to come with them. He'd only invited her to please Jeffrey, and because he hadn't wanted her to be embarrassed, but he had to admit he'd enjoyed her company. In fact, he'd enjoyed it a lot. The admission made him feel funny, as if enjoying being with Leslie was somehow disloyal to Joy.

"I really like her," Jeffrey was continuing eagerly. "Maybe she can have pizza with us *every* week."

"Now, son..." For a moment, Brian was at a loss. What could he say that would put a curb on

Jeffrey's enthusiasm without making it seem as if he didn't like Leslie? "I don't blame you for liking her," he added carefully, knowing this was delicate territory. "She's a very nice person."

"I told you."

"Yes, I know." Taking a deep breath, Brian plunged. "She, uh, sort of reminds me of Mom."

For a long moment, Jeffrey said nothing. Brian mentally kicked himself. He shouldn't have said anything about the similarity between the women. Maybe he'd upset Jeffrey. But then Jeffrey surprised him, saying in a stunned voice, "She *is* kind of like Mom, isn't she?" Under his breath, he added, "Cool."

Brian felt a bit stunned himself. Jeffrey's reaction was not what he'd imagined it would be, and he wasn't sure how to deal with it.

"So can we, Dad?"

"Can we what?"

"You know, ask Leslie to go for pizza with us *every* Friday?"

"Jeffrey, I know you like her, and I'm sure Leslie likes you, too, but she's an adult. She has lots of friends her own age and other things she wants to do on Friday nights."

"She didn't tonight," Jeffrey pointed out.

"I know, but that won't be true every Friday."

"Well, we could *ask* her, couldn't we?"

Brian sighed inwardly. Damn. He shouldn't have used other possible engagements as a reason for not including her in their Friday night pizzafest, because

Jeffrey was frustratingly logical. "Look, son, we're always truthful with each other, aren't we?"

"Yeah, sure, Dad."

"Well, the truth is, I look forward to going out with you on Friday nights. It's…kind of special, just you and me. I don't really want anyone else along."

Jeffrey frowned. "Oh."

Now Brian felt like a heel. But he couldn't have Jeffrey finagling for Leslie to become a permanent part of their Friday nights. Because no matter how much Brian might have enjoyed Leslie's company tonight, she was not someone whose friendship he wanted to cultivate or encourage.

He couldn't.

Because even though Jeffrey had seemed unconscious of Leslie's similarity to Joy, it was obvious to Brian that his son was looking for a substitute for his mother. But no matter how nice Leslie was, she was not his mother. And sooner or later, Jeffrey would have to face that fact. Brian felt it would hurt Jeffrey less to nip this situation in the bud than it would to allow the association to continue, then pull away later.

On the other hand, as long as Jeffrey was seeing Dr. Singer, he would be thrown into Leslie's orbit. And Brian certainly didn't want to stop Jeffrey's therapy, did he?

He could switch Jeffrey to another therapist. But switching therapists was a drastic step and might, in the end, cause Jeffrey more trauma than a continued association with Leslie ever would.

You don't have to make any decisions right now. Sleep on it.

Brian stifled a sigh. It was so damned hard being a single parent. There were so many decisions to make, and so many ramifications to each one. How was he supposed to know what the right thing was? Unfortunately, a lot of the time, he didn't. He just went by his gut instinct. And if that instinct turned out to be wrong, then he had to suffer the consequences.

But in this case, it would be Jeffrey suffering the consequences, and he had suffered enough. So Brian needed to be absolutely certain before he took any action.

"Where did you go last night? I called you a couple of times, then finally gave up."

It was early Saturday morning. As was their custom, Leslie and her best friend, Sandi Buchanan, were sitting in Leslie's kitchen drinking coffee prior to Sandi opening her real estate office.

"I went out for pizza after work, then ran some errands," Leslie said. "I didn't get home until after eight."

"Who'd you go out for pizza with?"

"One of Dr. Singer's patients."

"I thought all his patients were kids."

"They are." Leslie busied herself stirring her coffee and avoided Sandi's shrewd eyes. "His father was there, too," she said in as offhand a voice as she could manage.

"His father, huh? And is this father young? Old? Married? Good-looking?"

"Now, Sandi, don't go jumping to conclusions." Knowing Sandi, any suggestion of a date had her envisioning wedding bells. "It wasn't a date. Jeffrey, the patient, is the one who invited me, not his father."

Sandi reached for one of the bran muffins Leslie had set out. "Jeffrey..." she said thoughtfully. "Is that the kid whose mother died in London? The one you're always talking about?"

"Yes." Leslie reached for a muffin, too. "He's such a nice kid. He's had a rough time of it."

"So what's the father like?" Sandi split her muffin and buttered it. Her green eyes gleamed with curiosity.

Leslie should have known she couldn't distract Sandi by trying to turn the conversation to a discussion of Jeffrey. "He's a very nice man."

"That's it?"

"What more do you want me to say?"

"Tell me everything. How old is he? What does he look like? How did he act? Are you interested in him?"

"Sandi..."

"Come on, Leslie. Inquiring minds want to know," Sandi said with a grin. "You might as well give me all the nitty-gritty, 'cause if you don't, I'll just keep bugging you until you do." She ate some of her muffin.

Leslie rolled her eyes. "Okay, okay. I'd guess

he's in his late thirties or early forties. As to the rest of it...'' She ticked the items off on her fingers. ''He's nice-looking, he acted like a polite gentleman, and there's no percentage in being interested in him, so I didn't even think about it.'' *Liar. You did too think about it. Not only that, you dreamt about him!* Leslie wondered how Sandi would treat *that* little gem if she knew about it.

''Why is there no percentage in being interested in him?'' Sandi downed the rest of her muffin in one big bite. Several crumbs fell down the front of her apricot linen dress, and she absentmindedly brushed them off. Amber, Leslie's ten-year-old golden retriever, immediately lapped them up, then settled back down next to Leslie's feet.

''Because it's obvious he's still mourning the death of his wife,'' Leslie said.

''So?''

''*So?* So he's not ready for any kind of relationship. Any woman who was foolish enough to get involved with him would be fighting a losing battle, because he'd constantly be comparing her to his dead wife. And finding her wanting. I had enough of never measuring up when I was married to Elliott. Next time around—if there *is* a next time around— I want a man who thinks I'm the most wonderful woman on earth.''

''Elliott was a jerk.''

''That's beside the point.''

''No, it *is* the point. Don't judge everyone by your experience with Elliott. Why not give this other guy a chance? Hey, if he loved his wife that much, he's the kind of guy who knows how to commit. And believe me, there aren't that many of *those* around,'' she added dryly.

"Sandi, this *other guy*—whose name is Brian, by the way—is *not* interested in me. I told you. He's still *mourning* his wife. There's a world of difference between having loved her and still mourning her."

"He's gonna get over mourning her sometime, sweetie, and you might as well be the one to help him start over again. Believe me, if he's nice-looking and a nice guy—wait a minute. Does he have a good job?"

Leslie laughed. She couldn't help it. "Sandi, you're incorrigible."

"Thank you. Now answer my question."

"Yes," Leslie said with resignation. "He has a good job. He owns a construction company."

"There you go. Nice-looking. Nice person. Great prospects. Believe me, he won't be on the block for long. Women will be lining up, willing and eager to help him get over his loss."

"You make it sound like a meat market, or something."

Sandi got up and walked over to the counter where the coffeemaker sat. "Honey, that's exactly what it is," she said as she poured herself another cup. "And the first person there gets the choicest cut."

"Honestly…"

"Hey, you can scoff if you want to, but I'm just telling you the truth." She walked back to the table and sat down again.

"Look, even if I *were* interested in him, I'll probably never see him again."

"You don't have to wait for him to make a move. In this day and age, there's absolutely no reason you can't call him up and invite him to go somewhere. Buy some tickets for the next play at the Strand Street Theater and ask him to go."

"I can't just call him up." Even the thought of calling Brian Canfield was enough to give her the same kind of sick feeling in her stomach that she got when she looked down from a high place.

"Why not?"

"Because I just can't."

Sandi sighed dramatically while rolling her eyes heavenward. "Leslie, I give up. If you want to get married again, you're going to have to put forth a little effort. Show some initiative." When Leslie said nothing, Sandy went on. "Don't you *want* to get married again?"

It was a good question. One Leslie had asked herself many times. "Yes, I do," she said quietly. "But it's not my main goal in life. If I met someone compatible, someone who loved me for myself and wouldn't try to mold me into his idea of perfection the way Elliott did, then yes, it would be wonderful. But what I want more than marriage is a child."

"Unless you know something I don't, last time I heard, you can't accomplish that feat by yourself."

"I know. But I'm thinking of adopting."

In one of the few times since Leslie and Sandi had become good friends, Sandi seemed at a loss for words. Finally she said, "You serious?"

Leslie nodded.

"Wow. How long have you been thinking about this?"

"For a while now."

"Raising a kid on your own isn't easy. Look at Susan." Susan was Sandi's twin sister and, since her husband's death, was raising three children alone.

"I know."

"So are you thinking about a baby? Or an older kid?"

"Well, I'd love to get a baby, but I figure my chances will be better if I go for an older child."

"How come you've never mentioned this before?"

Leslie shrugged. "I don't know. I didn't want to talk about it until I'd thought about it some more."

For a few minutes, the two friends fell silent. Then, in a more subdued tone, Sandi said, "You talk to your mother about this?"

The question gave Leslie pause. Her relationship with her mother was complicated, filled with unresolved issues, even though since her divorce she had tried hard not to let her mother intimidate her. Even so, Leslie avoided conflict with her mother whenever possible, because she simply didn't need the stress.

"No," she said quietly, finally answering Sandi's question. "I haven't discussed it with her."

"You planning to? Or are you planning to just spring a kid on your parents with no warning?"

"Of course I'll tell them. But right now there's nothing to tell. I thought I'd look into adoption first, kind of see what my chances are, and then, if they look good, I'll talk to my parents."

Besides, there was no sense getting them riled up for nothing. Because even though they'd never discussed the subject, she knew her parents would not approve of their single daughter adopting a child. Her father might not have as much of a problem with it as her mother, because he wasn't as hung up on what people thought as Peggy was. But he wouldn't be wholeheartedly in support of such a drastic step, either.

Sandi nodded thoughtfully. "Yeah, that sounds like a good plan." She drained her coffee cup and rose. "Well, I'd better get going. Cathy is off today, so I'm playing receptionist as well as owner."

"Sandi, you work too hard."

"Can't help it. It's in my blood."

Leslie walked her to the door. They hugged, then Sandi said, "Greg and I are going to grill some salmon tonight. Why don't you come and have dinner with us?"

Leslie smiled. Sandi was so thoughtful. "That would be lovely. How about if I bring a salad?"

"Nope. Just bring yourself. About seven, okay?" Then Sandi grinned mischievously. "But if the handsome widower calls and offers you a more attractive alternative, say yes and don't worry about hurting our feelings."

"If you don't stop it, I'm going to be sorry I told you about him," Leslie said, but she couldn't help chuckling.

In answer, Sandi only winked.

Brian awakened later than usual Saturday morning because he'd spent a restless night. Restless nights were no stranger to him, not since Joy's death, but he hadn't had one for months and had mistakenly believed they were behind him.

Because he hadn't been able to sleep, he'd gotten up about two in the morning and walked out onto the second-floor deck, where he sat in one of the deck chairs and watched the moonlight play over the inky waters of the Gulf and listened to the soothing sound of the surf.

Brian hadn't grown up in Galveston. When his unmarried teenaged mother decided she couldn't cope with a baby—his father had deserted her during her pregnancy—she'd skipped out on him and his grandmother. His grandmother had raised him, and until he'd graduated from high school, he had rarely left the tiny west Texas town where they'd lived. Because there were no jobs there, Brian had moved to Houston, where he'd learned the construction trade while going to the University of Houston at night.

Those had been tough years. He'd had no time

for a social life, and even if he had, he had no money, for every spare penny was sent to his grandmother, who could no longer work and didn't get enough in Social Security benefits to support herself.

It was only after his grandmother died, when Brian was twenty-four, that he'd been able to afford to take a girl out once in a while. Six months after his grandmother's death, he'd met Joy. And he'd never wanted another woman since.

Joy had been a Galveston native. And when they married, Galveston was where she wanted them to live. "I'm sorry," she'd said. "I know you probably think I'm such a mama's girl, but I'm their only child, and I want to live near my parents."

Brian hadn't had a problem with living close to her parents. He'd always envied people who were part of a close-knit family, and now that his grandmother was gone, he craved that sense of belonging more than ever. Marrying Joy, being close to her parents, whom he already loved and felt close to, would give him far more than he'd be giving up. Besides, he could work in construction anywhere.

He'd had no idea how much he would love living on the island. But love it he did. And when he was troubled, as he had been last night—hell, as he *still* was this morning—sitting where he could see and hear the water had always helped him think.

Ever since they'd left her, he'd been thinking about Leslie Marlowe. Just before dawn, he'd finally faced the fact that Jeffrey wasn't the only Canfield male to feel an attraction to her. Immediately, he was nearly overwhelmed with guilt.

How could he be attracted to Leslie? What kind of a man was he? Joy had only been dead a little over a year, and he had loved her with all his heart. In fact, if he could have traded places with her, died instead of her, he would have. Yet, not much more than a year later, he was feeling an attraction to another woman.

It's only because she reminds you of Joy, he told himself. But she wasn't Joy. There would never be another Joy.

He reminded himself of this fact once again on Saturday morning as he made coffee and mixed up pancake batter for his and Jeffrey's breakfast.

He had just poured himself a cup of coffee when Brian heard Jeffrey coming downstairs. Jeffrey was already dressed for the day in khaki shorts and a T-shirt.

"Good morning," Brian said, wiping his mind free so that Jeffrey wouldn't suspect the turmoil his father had been feeling.

"Mornin'." Jeffrey opened the refrigerator and took out a carton of orange juice.

Brian cooked their pancakes, then joined his son at the table. They ate in silence for a while, then Jeffrey said, "I was thinking, Dad, I know you don't want Leslie to go with us on Friday nights, but could we ask her to go to Astroworld with us next Saturday?"

Brian finished chewing, then said, "We'll see." It was the only thing he could think to say.

"She doesn't have any kids, so she pro'bly never gets to go to Astroworld," Jeffrey persisted. He shoveled half a pancake in his mouth.

It was on the tip of Brian's tongue to point out that Leslie might not be crazy about amusement parks, but he decided it would be wiser to keep from prolonging the discussion, so he simply made a non-committal sound, picked up the remote, and turned on the small TV they kept in the kitchen. He switched the channel to CNN and hoped Jeffrey would drop the subject.

His ploy worked. Jeffrey stuffed the last of his pancakes into his mouth, then downed the remainder of his milk. "I'm gonna go do some stuff on the computer," he said as he pushed his chair back and stood.

"Okay."

After Jeffrey headed for his bedroom, Brian knew he had to make a decision about Leslie soon, because it was obvious Jeffrey would continue to push to have her included in whatever they did.

All weekend long, the subject was on Brian's mind. And finally, on Sunday night, he came to a decision. He'd been approaching the problem from the wrong end. What he needed to do was talk to Leslie and explain the situation. When she understood why Jeffrey had gotten so attached to her, she would probably work with Brian to discourage any more contact than was absolutely necessary. Then he would talk to Dr. Singer so he would be aware of the problem, too. For a moment he wondered if he should reverse the order and talk to Dr. Singer first. No, he wanted Leslie to know the situation before he talked to Dr. Singer. Otherwise, she might feel he was somehow criticizing her or going behind her back.

Feeling relieved at having a course of action, he suddenly wanted to get out of the house. "Want to go see a movie tonight?" he asked Jeffrey.

"Sure!"

"Let's look in the paper and see what's playing." Brian picked up the newspaper and was reading it when the phone rang.

Jeffrey, who had been lying on his stomach in front of the TV, jumped up. "I'll get it."

A few seconds later, Brian heard him say, "Grandma! Hi!"

Brian smiled. Last year, when it had only been a couple of months after Joy's death, Hank and Theresa Paladino had skipped their annual summer trip to Canada, even though, with Hank's heart condition, the Galveston summers were bad for him. But this year Brian had encouraged them to go. He knew how much Hank loved the fishing and the cabin they always rented. There were other retirees who went to the same area, and he knew his in-laws missed seeing their friends, too. So a week ago, they'd gone.

He listened to Jeffrey's end of the conversation for a while. "We went to Pizza Heaven," Jeffrey was saying, and Brian knew Theresa had asked him about the previous evening. "Leslie went with us. It was cool."

Brian froze. Although having Leslie with them had been Jeffrey's idea and it wasn't a date or anything close to it, he couldn't help the guilt that flooded him. What would Theresa say? He dreaded having to explain who Leslie was and why she was with them, because no matter what he said, he knew they would wonder. The Paladinos had taken the death of their only child very hard, and Brian knew that if he ever *did* begin seeing another woman, it would be difficult for them. He wished Jeffrey hadn't said anything, but it was too late now.

Jeffrey walked into the living room and handed Brian the portable phone. "Gran wants to talk to you, too."

"Hi, Theresa," Brian said. "You two having a good time?"

"Yes, but I wish you and Jeffrey were here with us," Theresa said. "I miss you already." She'd done her level best to persuade Brian to take a week or two off and come with them, but Brian had resisted. He figured he'd take Jeffrey somewhere in August just before school started again.

"The month will go fast," he said.

"Yes, I know. I was telling Jeffrey we tried to call you last night. But he said you went for pizza with one of his friends."

Brian knew he should correct her. He knew she thought Leslie was Jeffrey's age. But for some reason, he hesitated, and then she began talking again, and the moment passed. "Then Dad and I went over to the Karrs' cabin to eat fish and play bridge, and when we got back it was too late to call again."

"So how *is* the fishing? Hank catching a lot?"

"Oh, you know him. He throws most of them back."

Brian laughed. His father-in-law was an old softy. He didn't even like killing spiders, let alone fish. "Man should never kill more than he can eat," he'd told Brian once, and Brian agreed.

"So what are you two planning for the rest of the weekend?" she asked.

"Not a whole lot. We were thinking of taking in a movie tonight."

"That sounds like fun."

They talked a while longer, then Theresa said, "Well, I suppose I should let you go. Let me just say goodbye to Jeffrey."

After they'd hung up, Brian went back to the newspaper, and he and Jeffrey talked about the merits of the available movies, finally deciding on an action–adventure film. But Brian's mind wasn't on the movies. His mind was on his in-laws and the way he'd deceived them.

Maybe he hadn't deceived them purposely, but the end result was the same.

Why hadn't he told Theresa who Leslie was? After all, there was nothing wrong in having invited her to have pizza with them. Yet not telling Theresa had made it seem as if there *was*.

That was stupid.

Brian decided that, if the situation ever arose again, he would not hide behind a half-truth. He would explain about Leslie immediately.

But the situation *wouldn't* come up again. It couldn't. Because just the fact that he'd felt funny about telling Theresa about Leslie was proof that sharing even the one pizza with Leslie Marlowe had been a huge mistake.

Chapter Four

Leslie thought about her conversation with Sandi off and on all day Saturday and again on Saturday night after she got home from dinner at Sandi and Greg's.

She wished she could be the kind of woman who was bold enough to take the initiative with a man, but even if she had been, she knew she would never do so with Brian. Because if she *did* take a chance, call him up and invite him to go somewhere as Sandi had suggested, and he refused…she would be totally mortified.

It wasn't as if he were just some stranger, and she never had to see him again. As long as Jeffrey was a patient of Dr. Singer's, there was always the possibility of running into Brian.

No. Leslie could never risk that.

Just forget about him, she told herself. It's easy for Sandi to talk. Sandi's been married so long, she's forgotten what it's like out here in the real world. Besides, you already decided he comes with too much emotional baggage....

But no matter how many times she told herself all of this, she couldn't seem to get Brian out of her mind. The trouble was, there weren't a lot of men out there as appealing as he was. That combination of rugged, outdoorsy male, loving father, and wounded widower was a potent one, and Leslie knew Sandi was right: sooner or later, women *would* be vying for the position of the second Mrs. Canfield. In fact, for all Leslie knew, there was a potential Mrs. Canfield on the scene right now.

For just a few moments, Leslie allowed herself to imagine being married to Brian...being a mother to Jeffrey. But then she ruthlessly pushed the images from her mind. She had to stop this. There was no chance, *no chance at all,* that she would ever even come close to a relationship with Brian Canfield, nor did she really want to, at least not while he was still trying to get over the death of his wife.

Anyway, all you did was eat pizza with them! And the invitation to do that had not come from Brian. It had come from Jeffrey.

Brian Canfield will never ask you out.

It was a struggle, but she had finally managed to put him out of her mind by the time she was on her way to her parents' home for Sunday dinner. Unless they were out of town, the members of the Marlowe family always had Sunday dinner together. Sometimes Leslie resented her virtual command appearance, but it did give her a chance to see her brother, Nick, and his family on a fairly regular basis.

She smiled, thinking of Nick. At thirty-nine, he was four years older than Leslie, but the two had always been close. She liked Nick's wife Michelle, too, and she doted on her brother's three children.

But when she arrived and walked to the family room at the back of her parents' house, where everyone normally congregated, the room was empty save for her father, who sat reading the Sunday paper in his leather recliner. He looked up and smiled, then slowly rose. A tall, thin man in his early sixties, he had a perpetual tan from his yearlong love affair with golf.

"Am I the first one here?" She walked over and gave him a hug.

"It's just going to be you, your mother and me, I'm afraid," her father said. "Nick and Michelle and the kids went to New Braunfels for the weekend."

Leslie tried not to sound as disappointed as she felt. "Oh, too bad." She hated the Sundays when her brother and his family weren't there, because then there was no buffer between Leslie and her mother, whose entire focus would now rest on Leslie.

Quelling a sigh, she laid her purse on the window seat that overlooked the backyard. "Where *is* Mom?" The family room was divided from the kitchen by a bar, and Leslie could see that her mother wasn't there.

"She went upstairs. She'll be down in a minute."

Leslie wandered out to the kitchen and looked inside the two pots on the stove. One held broccoli, the other mashed potatoes. Through the glass door of the oven, she could see chicken breasts baking. Peggy Marlowe was not an imaginative cook, preferring to spend any spare time she might have playing bridge or tennis.

Leslie took a glass out of the cupboard and poured herself a glass of water. Just as she was returning the cold water jug to the refrigerator, she heard her mother's light footsteps on the uncarpeted oak stairs.

"Hello, darling," her mother said as she entered the kitchen. She raised her cheek for Leslie's kiss.

As always, when Leslie saw her mother, she felt a familiar mixture of love and irritation. "Hello, Mother. What a pretty dress."

Leslie had learned long ago that her mother not only expected compliments on her appearance and clothing, but would be highly miffed if they were not forthcoming. "Is it new?"

"Yes," her mother said, smiling. "I bought it at Neiman's the last time I was in Houston." She smoothed down the skirt of the peach linen dress, which looked impeccable on her petite figure.

Leslie had always felt like an elephant next to her mother, who at five foot two was a good eight inches shorter than her daughter. Leslie took after her father's family, inheriting both his height and auburn hair. Nick resembled Peggy's family, the majority of whom were blond with blue eyes.

Peggy eyed Leslie's outfit—tan slacks and a pale yellow summer weight sweater. "You didn't go to church in pants, I hope."

"No," Leslie said quietly, "I changed before coming over."

Her mother nodded, and Leslie knew she disapproved. Well, what else was new? Peggy always disapproved of the things Leslie did, but in this instance, Leslie didn't care. It was too warm—not to mention uncomfortable—to stay in panty hose and a dress if she didn't have to. After all, it was only Sunday dinner with her parents, and if her mother didn't like it, well, she could just lump it. The thought made her smile. Wouldn't Dr. Dixon, her former therapist, be proud of her? Standing up to her mother, even in her thoughts, was a giant step ahead of where Leslie had once been.

For the next few minutes, as she helped her mother put the food on the dining-room table, they didn't talk much, for which Leslie was grateful. If they didn't talk, Leslie couldn't get mad, and if she didn't get mad, she couldn't get in trouble. But the reprieve didn't last long. Once the three of them were sitting down and had said grace, her mother turned to Leslie and said, in exactly the same words she used every Sunday, "Well, how was your week?"

"Really busy." This was Leslie's standard answer.

"What did you do besides work?" This, too, was a routine question.

"Oh, the usual things. Glee club practice Tuesday, the children's shelter Wednesday, and dinner with Sandi and Greg last night." Leslie ate a bite of her chicken and waited for the inevitable rejoinder.

"You know, darling," her mother said a few moments later, "if you had a different kind of job, you might actually meet some eligible men once in a while. Maybe even have a date occasionally."

This, too, was a standard opinion rendered almost every time Leslie and her mother were together. "I have no desire to change jobs, Mother, you know that. I love what I do." She purposely ignored the date remark.

"Aside from the fact that you'll never meet anyone working for a children's psychologist, your father could really use you at the agency, couldn't you, Ross?"

Leslie's father owned an insurance agency, and for years, her mother had been trying to get Leslie to go to work there.

"Now, Peggy, we've had this conversation before," Leslie's father said mildly. He surreptitiously raised his eyebrows at Leslie.

"And we'll continue to have it," her mother said, not in the least deterred by his lack of support, "until Leslie listens to reason."

Leslie sighed. "Mother, please..."

"Please, what?" Peggy said. "You're not getting any younger, you know."

"None of us are," Leslie said dryly.

"Don't get smart with me, young lady."

Leslie put down her fork. Met her mother's eyes. Sighed. "Look, Mother, I'm sorry. I wasn't trying to be smart. Really. But you refuse to listen to me. I am perfectly happy with my life just the way it is." She ignored the guilty twinge reminding her she *wasn't* happy with her life just the way it was. Hadn't she, in fact, told Sandi only yesterday that she planned to investigate adopting a child? And hadn't she, just this morning, been spinning day-dreams around Brian Canfield?

"Well," Peggy said stiffly, "I don't believe you. No normal woman of your age could possibly be happy in a dead-end job. I'd think you'd be concerned about your future. Especially since it doesn't look as if you'll ever get married again."

"Peg..." Leslie's father said, a warning note in his tone.

"I just wish that for once in your life, you'd listen," Peggy said, totally ignoring him.

Leslie wanted to point out that once in her life, she *had* listened, because her mother had been very much in favor of Leslie's marrying Elliott. And that decision had been the worst one of her life. But while she was still trying to decide if she really wanted to escalate this discussion into all-out war, her father intervened.

"Peggy, that's enough. You've made your point.

Leslie's an adult. She can make her own decisions. So let's drop the subject.''

Leslie sent her father a grateful look. When he spoke to her mother in that particular authoritative tone, she always gave way. Today was no exception. She contented herself with a sigh and a roll of the eyes, then devoted herself to her meal and much more pleasant conversation about the trip to Italy she and Leslie's father had booked for the fall.

Nevertheless, Leslie felt drained by the time she left and she vowed that on future Sundays, she would check with Nick and Michelle, and if they weren't going to be at her parents', she would find a reason to stay away, too, because she simply couldn't handle many more of her mother's harangues. She knew that one of these days, she was going to explode and tell her mother exactly how she felt.

I just want to make my own choices and live my own life. Why can't she understand that? She's lived hers the way she wanted to. Why is it so hard for her to accord me that same privilege?

But as always, there was no answer to the question.

Monday morning was one of the busiest Leslie had ever seen. Not only did Dr. Singer have a full schedule of appointments, but the telephone also rang nonstop.

At ten o'clock, she felt as if she'd already worked

a full day. She sighed when two lines rang at once, putting the first on hold to grab the second.

"Leslie?"

Her pulse quickened. "Yes?"

"Hi, it's Brian Canfield."

"Hi, Brian. I'm sorry, but do you mind holding for a minute?"

"No. Of course not."

She hurriedly dispatched the other call, then punched the button for his call. She told herself not to get excited. He was probably calling for Dr. Singer.

"How can I help you?" she said.

"I was wondering. Are you free for lunch today?"

The question was so unexpected, it took a few seconds for her to compose herself and answer without stammering. "Yes."

"There's something I'd like to discuss with you, and I thought maybe we could talk at lunch."

"Sure. That would be fine."

"What time do you normally go?"

"The office closes at noon, but you'd better give me about fifteen minutes more today. It's been a really busy morning."

"Okay. I'll be there at twelve-fifteen."

They hung up, and Leslie sat there staring at the phone. There was something he wanted to discuss. What could it be? Was it something to do with Jeffrey? But if that was the case, why wouldn't he talk to Dr. Singer?

For the remainder of the morning Leslie tried to figure out what it was Brian wanted to talk to her about, but she couldn't imagine.

A few minutes after twelve, when the last patient of the morning left, Leslie switched the phone over to the answering service, then raced into the ladies' to freshen her makeup and hair. She looked down at her beige dress and wished she'd worn something nicer to work today.

By twelve-ten she was back at her desk, pretending to be absorbed in a file so that Brian wouldn't suspect how anxiously she was awaiting his arrival. She told herself to stay calm and cool, because his invitation to lunch had no personal significance whatsoever.

Even so, when the door opened, her heart gave an involuntary leap as Brian walked in. Dressed in jeans and an open-necked navy shirt, he looked very attractive. Too attractive, she thought distractedly, her heart picking up speed.

"Hi," he said, smiling.

"Hi." Good grief, he certainly had the ability to disconcert her.

"Ready to go?"

"Uh-huh." She took her purse out of her bottom drawer and stood.

"Is there anyplace special you'd like to go?"

"Anyplace will be a treat for me. I usually just go to the little luncheonette downstairs." Her heart was still beating too fast, and she told herself to calm down. It was only lunch.

"Do you like Mexican food?"

"Of course I like Mexican food. I'm a Texan." That was better. That's the way she wanted to sound: witty and relaxed.

"How about Pepé's Cantina, then?" he said, naming a popular Mexican restaurant near the Strand.

"That sounds great."

When they walked outside, they were hit by a blast of heat, and Leslie realized summer had snuck up on her when she wasn't looking. Today the temperature must have been close to ninety. She could feel perspiration beading her neck before they even reached Brian's truck. How lovely, she thought, wishing she was one of those women who always looked cool and perfectly put together.

"Sorry about the truck," he said, helping her up into the cab, "but I have to pick up some supplies on the way back to work."

"I don't mind."

He smiled. "But I did clean it out in your honor."

"I appreciate that," she said, returning his smile.

As he pulled out of the parking lot, she speculated about what he might want to discuss. Had something happened with Jeffrey? Brian didn't seem upset, so whatever was on his mind, it couldn't be anything too bad.

"Where's Jeffrey today?" she asked, remembering that Brian's housekeeper was gone this week.

"A friend asked him to spend the day. They were going to go to Sea World."

"Oh, that's nice."

"Yes, it is. Jeffrey doesn't get to do many things like that when his grandparents are gone."

His words reminded Leslie of what Sandi had said—how difficult it was to raise a child on your own.

"Maybe I'll reciprocate later in the week," Brian continued. "Take them to NASA or something. Or maybe drive up to Houston for an Astros game."

Because his statement required no answer, Leslie said nothing more, and they lapsed into silence for the remainder of the drive to the restaurant. Leslie wished she knew what it was Brian wanted to discuss with her, but it didn't look as if he was going to tell her until they got to the restaurant.

Pepé's Cantina was housed in an attractive, bright building with Mexican tile floors and lots of windows. When they arrived, it was crowded, but Pepé himself came out to say hello to Brian, and they were immediately led to a window table in a far corner.

"I feel honored," Leslie said. "From what I understand, Pepé doesn't make a fuss over just anyone."

Brian smiled. "We're old friends. I built this place for him."

"Ah, that explains it." She looked around. "It's a lovely building."

"Thanks."

Their waiter put a basket of warm chips and a bowl of salsa on their table and took their drink orders. After he left, Brian said, "I know you're wondering what's on my mind."

"Well, yes."

"It's Jeffrey."

"I figured as much."

He hesitated. "I'm sure you realize Jeffrey is very taken with you."

Leslie smiled. "The feeling is mutual."

"From the very beginning, I've been wondering what it was about you that had made such an impression on him."

"I've wondered the same thing myself. All I know is, there was an instant connection between us."

Brian nodded thoughtfully. Before he could answer, their waiter appeared with their drinks. Leslie stirred sweetener and lemon into her iced tea and waited for Brian to continue.

"When I saw you," he said after the waiter left again, "I knew."

Leslie frowned. "Knew what?"

"Knew why Jeffrey felt that connection you described." He met her eyes squarely. "You see, there's something about you that is very like his mother."

Leslie stared at him, stunned. "You…you mean I *look* like her?"

He shook his head. "No, not really. You do have almost the same color hair, but that's the only real physical similarity. Her eyes were much lighter, like Jeffrey's. And she was little, whereas you're tall. It's hard to describe, but the similarity has more to do with the way you talk to people. The way you smile. Your smile is very much like hers.'' As he said this, a shadow passed over his face, and he looked away.

Leslie knew he was remembering, and that the memories still hurt. She had a strong urge to reach out and touch his hand, to offer whatever comfort she could, but she resisted, because he was, after all, little more than a stranger, and he might not appreciate her crossing that line. Instead, she drank some of her iced tea and sat patiently.

''I'm concerned,'' he added after a few moments had passed. His eyes met hers again. ''Jeffrey's come a long way. I don't want to do anything that would cause him to lose ground.''

Leslie mulled over what he'd said. He was probably right to be concerned, she admitted reluctantly. She'd worked for Dr. Singer long enough to realize the potential harm of emotional transference. She nodded thoughtfully. ''I wish I'd known.''

He shrugged. ''How could you? I'm not even sure Jeffrey was aware of the similarities between you and his mother. Not on a conscious level, anyhow.''

As he was speaking, their waiter reappeared. ''Ready to order?'' he said.

''Maybe we'd better,'' Brian said.

So for the next few minutes they scanned the menu and placed their orders.

''I think you should talk to Dr. Singer about this,'' Leslie asked when their waiter had once more left.

"I'm planning to, but I wanted you to know what was going on first."

"Is there something you think I can do? I'll be glad to do anything you feel is necessary."

"I don't know. I've been thinking about it all weekend. You're not his mother, no matter what he might wish. Frankly, I'm worried that continuing to be in your company so much might not be a good idea."

Leslie couldn't help feeling a pang. "But as long as he's going to Dr. Singer, he will be around me," she pointed out. "It's unavoidable."

"I know."

"Are you thinking of switching therapists, then?"

"I've thought about it. But I'm afraid that might hurt Jeffrey more in the long run. I guess I'll leave it up to Dr. Singer."

It hurt Leslie to think she might never see Jeffrey again. Yet she understood Brian's dilemma, because he was right. She *wasn't* Jeffrey's mother and never would be.

By now their food had come: chilis rellenos for Brian and Baja shrimp tacos for Leslie. Fragrant aromas wafted from the steaming plates.

As they began to eat, Leslie thought about fate and how chancy it could be. Fate had brought Brian Canfield and his son into her life, and fate could just as easily take them away again. And if it did, she would miss more than just Jeffrey. She would also miss this big man sitting opposite her. It was true that she hardly knew him, but what she did know about him was enough to tell her that he could have been important to her.

They ate silently for a while, both lost in their thoughts.

About halfway through their meal, Brian said, "You know, I can't really blame Jeffrey for trying to hang on to his mother. It's still hard for *me* to believe she's gone. There have been times when I was sure that any moment I'd wake up and find out it had all been a dream. That she was still alive."

Leslie nodded. In a way, she understood exactly what Brian meant. Even though she and Elliott had been divorced, which was different from being parted by death, she had suffered some of the same disbelief and shock. The same sense of unreality.

"It's ironic how things work out," he said. "My father ran out on my mother before I was born, and when I was just a toddler, she dumped me with my grandmother and I never saw her again. I vowed that when I had kids of my own, they would have an entirely different kind of life—one with a mother and a father—and they would always feel secure." He grimaced.

"What happened wasn't your fault."

"I know. But it doesn't change the end result. Joy is still gone."

"Would you like to tell me about her?" Leslie asked softly.

"You don't want to hear—"

"But I do," she said.

He studied her face, then apparently seeing her

sincerity, began speaking softly. "I fell in love with her the first time I saw her. It was on the University of Houston campus. During the summer. It was early evening, and she was standing on one of the paths, talking to a couple of girls. Joy's hair was long and curly then, and it was blowing all around her face. She kept pushing it away, you know, the way a woman does, kind of absentmindedly. Her eyes were all shiny, and she had this laugh…God, it was a wonderful laugh. She made me want to laugh, too. I kept looking at her, and I just knew she was the one I'd been waiting for."

He was smiling, his eyes soft with his memories. "So what did you do?" Leslie prompted.

The smile turned into a grin. "I walked over and introduced myself. I'd never done anything like that in my life. I just said, 'Hi, I'm Brian Canfield, and I'm going to marry you.' The other girls giggled and carried on, but Joy didn't. She tilted her head and gave me this funny little quizzical look, studying me for a while. Then she said, well, if that was the case, we'd better start getting acquainted, didn't I think?"

Leslie couldn't imagine having so much poise and confidence that you could answer that way. "How old were you then?"

"I was twenty-four, Joy was twenty-one. Twenty-one going on ninety, as her father was fond of saying. Wise beyond her years. You could go to her with a problem, and she could always put it into perspective for you."

Leslie nodded. That's the way Sandi was and it

was one of the qualities that had most attracted Leslie to her.

"But she was also lots of fun," he continued. "She loved to have a good time. Loved to do things on the spur of the moment. People were drawn to her."

Leslie smiled. "She sounds wonderful."

"She was," he said softly.

The expression on his face caused an ache in the vicinity of Leslie's heart. What must it be like to be loved the way Joy Canfield had obviously been loved?

What do you mean, was? *He still loves her....*

For it was very clear to Leslie that Jeffrey was not the only one who hadn't gotten over the loss of Joy. Brian still grieved. But that was natural. After all, it had only been a little over a year since her death. And when you had the kind of relationship that Brian and his wife had obviously had, you didn't get it over it quickly.

Knowing she had to say something more, she said, "She also sounds like someone I would have liked a lot."

"Funny you should say that, because I was thinking earlier today that Joy would have liked you a lot, too."

His words gave Leslie a warm feeling. He'd been thinking about her.

Well, you dodo, she scolded herself, *of course he was thinking about you. Didn't he just tell you he's worried about Jeffrey's feelings for you? Don't read more into this than he meant.* "What a nice thing to say. Thank you."

For a long moment, nothing more was said. And then, in a choked voice, he said, "She was pregnant, you know."

Leslie's hand went involuntarily to her mouth. She swallowed, hard. "No," she whispered, "I didn't know."

Pain suffused his face. "We hadn't told anyone. Not even her parents. We'd wanted another child for a long time. She was just four months pregnant, and the trip to London was to celebrate. We were planning to tell her folks when we got back. We knew they'd be as thrilled as we were."

Dear God.

"They still don't know."

"You never told them?"

He shrugged. "Why hurt them any more than they were already hurt? They're really nice people, and they've had a rough time. Joy was their only child."

Not telling them about the pregnancy was a very kind thing to do, but what a terrible burden to carry around alone, she thought.

After that, neither one of them felt like finishing their food. In unspoken agreement, they left the restaurant and drove back to Leslie's office in silence.

When Brian pulled into the parking lot, Leslie turned to him. "Thank you for lunch. I enjoyed it."

"I don't see how," he answered with a rueful smile. "I wasn't exactly a fun companion."

"Please, don't feel bad about talking to me. I—I feel honored that you confided in me."

His eyes met hers.

So blue, she thought.

"I appreciate you listening. And I also appreciate you understanding about Jeffrey. You're a nice person."

Leslie forced herself to answer casually when what she really wanted to do was tell him she thought he was the nicest man she'd ever met. "Speaking of Jeffrey, do you want me to look and see what times Dr. Singer has available this week for you to come and talk with him?"

"Would you?"

"Certainly. And if you like, I'll just call your office later and let you know."

"That would be great." He reached over and squeezed her hand. "Thanks again."

"Anytime."

They said goodbye, and she got out of the truck. As she walked into the office building, she resisted the impulse to turn around and watch him leave.

Chapter Five

All afternoon, anytime Leslie's mind wasn't occupied with work, she thought about Brian. Not just about their lunch together and the things he'd said, but Brian himself. And she couldn't help comparing him to Elliott.

What would her life have been like if she'd married someone like Brian, instead of Elliott? Leslie couldn't imagine. To be with a man who thought you were wonderful, who didn't try to make you into something you weren't, who didn't constantly tell you how worthless you were, in subtle and not-so-subtle ways....

Leslie remembered the first time she had met Elliott for lunch after they were married. He had taken her to Gaido's. She'd been thrilled, thinking he wanted to make their lunch date special. Months later she'd realized the only reason he'd chosen Gaido's was because that was where his clients and competitors lunched, the place to see and be seen.

She had worn a dark green wool suit—one Elliott had handpicked on a shopping trip to Houston. Elliott had chosen most of her clothes because he thought her taste in clothing was inferior to his. And Leslie had been so young—only nineteen when they were married—and she'd had so little confidence in herself, she never questioned his judgment or his opinions.

She had dressed and applied her makeup and styled her hair with the utmost care. In those days, Elliott's approval meant everything. She remembered how self-conscious she'd felt as she entered the restaurant and walked slowly toward his table. How she'd literally held her breath while she waited to hear the words of praise that would tell her she had passed the first hurdle of the day successfully.

"You should have worn your brown alligator heels," he murmured as he leaned forward to kiss her cheek. "Why didn't you?"

She looked down at her black suede pumps. "I—I thought—"

"That's just the problem..." Elliott smiled his most charming smile for the benefit of the other diners, but his gray eyes were cold, so cold as they met hers. "You *thought*."

Her lower lip trembled, even though she knew Elliott hated her tendency to get teary-eyed when he criticized her. She was so stupid. She couldn't seem to do anything right. No wonder he got exasperated with her.

Lips tight with disapproval, he pulled out her chair, bending close as he helped seat her. He hissed under his breath. "Smile, dammit. What is *wrong* with you that I can't say a word without you getting upset?"

She'd tried. She'd tried so hard. But for the remainder of their lunch, he found fault with everything she said and everything she did. And all the while, she had to smile and pretend that everything was fine, that her husband wasn't decimating her with his wintry eyes and his hurtful words.

That luncheon was only a harbinger of the years ahead. There was no pleasing Elliott. And the harder she tried, the more she seemed to fail. Her taste in clothing, her taste in friends, her taste in music, books, movies...all were found lacking. And her opinions? They were dismissed out of hand unless she was agreeing with Elliott's views. Even then, she had to be careful. If she said too much, he would accuse her of never having an opinion of her own.

It wasn't until she'd entered therapy after her divorce that she'd begun to understand why she'd stayed with Elliott for as long as she had. She now realized it was common for people who had unresolved issues with their parents to pick a spouse with many of the same characteristics. Still, even given her lack of confidence in herself and her predilection to try to please at any cost, it still sickened her to remember what a complete doormat she'd been during the five years they'd been married.

There were still times she wondered if she would ever have had the courage to make the break, because their marriage didn't end by her choice. Elliott was the one who had walked out.

It happened when she returned home from her hospital stay after her fourth and final miscarriage. She'd been devastated, knowing it would be hopeless to try again. She had prayed that just this once Elliott would be different. That he would be sympathetic and understanding. That he would take her in his arms and comfort her and tell her it was all right, that he loved her and they could be happy, anyway.

Instead he came into the bedroom while she was unpacking her overnight bag and said without preamble, "I'm leaving you, Leslie."

She slowly turned around. "Leaving me?" she parroted numbly.

"Yes. I want children. And you can't have them."

And with that, he left.

Remembering, she sighed. The hurt had disappeared long ago. Her therapy, her job, the friends she'd made and the life she'd built, had all contributed to changing her from a pitiful, weak girl into a strong, confident woman.

She'd eventually come to realize that her unhappiness in her marriage was just as much her fault as it was Elliott's. After all, you can't be victimized unless you permit it, and she had not only permitted it, she had encouraged it by never standing up to Elliott.

Still, she couldn't imagine Brian Canfield ever treating his wife the way Elliott had treated her, even if she'd had Leslie's personality. She couldn't imagine Brian ever treating *any* woman that way.

Once again, she thought how different her life would have been if she'd met someone like Brian Canfield first. Someone who would have cherished her and helped her grow. Someone who would have respected her.

Regret filled her. If only circumstances were different with Brian. If only he were ready to find love again. But circumstances *weren't* different. He wasn't ready. And maybe he never would be.

Just before five, Leslie's mother called.

"Mom?" Leslie said. "Is something wrong?" Her mother never called her at work, so it must be important.

"Does something have to be wrong for me to call my daughter?"

Leslie sighed. "No, of course not."

"I was just curious, that's all. Lorene Cuttler tells me she saw you having lunch at Pepé's with a good-looking man today."

Leslie grimaced. Lorene Cuttler was one of her mother's bosom friends and the biggest gossip in the county.

"Well? Who is he? Anyone I know?"

"I doubt it. He's the father of one of Dr. Singer's patients."

"And just how long has this been going on? And why is your mother the last to know?"

Her mother's voice was playful, but Leslie knew she was dead serious.

"I didn't tell you because there's nothing to tell," Leslie said quietly, determined not to let her mother upset her. "It wasn't a social lunch. He simply wanted to talk to me about his son."

"Why you? Why not Dr. Singer?"

Leslie counted to ten. "Mother, please. You know I can't discuss Dr. Singer's patients with you. You're just going to have to trust me when I say my lunch today wasn't social. Okay?" Leslie knew her voice revealed her impatience, but she didn't try to disguise it. "Now, if you don't mind, I have to go. I have a call coming in on the other line. I'll see you Sunday." Before her mother could say anything else, Leslie hung up.

She knew she had probably infuriated her mother. Peggy was not used to being dismissed. She was used to doing the dismissing. But right now Leslie didn't care.

And on Sunday if her mother tried to pump her about Brian, she might just tell her mother to mind her own business.

"So did you have a good time today?" Brian asked.

Jeffrey buckled his seat belt. "Yeah, it was cool."

It was six o'clock and, as prearranged, Brian had just picked Jeffrey up from his friend's house.

"What did you like the best?"

"The dolphins."

Brian smiled. "The dolphins are my favorites, too."

"I got to pet one of them. That was *really* cool."

Jeffrey continued to jabber about Sea World for the remainder of the drive home. When they got there, he immediately took off for his room, and Brian went about making preparations for their dinner. He had removed the meat loaf from the freezer that morning, so now he washed two potatoes and put them in the microwave to bake, then took the lettuce out of the refrigerator to wash for a salad.

Forty minutes later, the table was set, and he called Jeffrey downstairs.

"Can we watch 'Wheel'?" Jeffrey asked.

Normally, Brian didn't like the TV set to be on during their dinner hour, but today he wasn't much in the mood for talking—he'd already talked far too much, he thought wryly—so he said, "Sure," and picked up the remote.

By the time "Wheel of Fortune" was over, they were finished with their dinner.

"Dad?" Jeffrey said, "Did you think about Astroworld?"

"What about Astroworld?"

"You know. Asking Leslie to go with us."

If Brian had hoped Jeffrey would forget about asking Leslie to accompany them to Astroworld, it was now obvious he was mistaken. It was also clear that no matter what had prompted Jeffrey's attachment to Leslie, it was very real and obviously important to the boy.

"Son," he answered gently, "I know you like Leslie a lot, but she has her own life to live. I doubt she'd want to go to Astroworld with us."

"Yes, she would," Jeffrey said stubbornly. "She likes us. I know she does." He frowned. "Don't you like her, too?"

Brian hesitated. "Yes," he finally said, "I like her, too."

Later, after Jeffrey had helped clean up the kitchen and gone upstairs to mess around on his computer, Brian thought about Leslie and their conversation at lunch. He couldn't remember when he'd talked so openly to anyone. He still couldn't believe he'd told Leslie about the baby. But there was just something about her that encouraged confidences. He'd looked into those warm brown eyes, and the words had just poured out.

He thought about Jeffrey and his question about whether Brian liked Leslie. He hadn't been completely truthful with Jeffrey when he'd answered. Because the complete truth was, Brian didn't just like Leslie.

He liked her far too much.

That night Leslie called Sandi, ostensibly just to chat, but down deep she knew the real reason was she wanted to talk about Brian again.

"So what's up?" Sandi said, astute as always.

"You know the man I was telling you about on Saturday?"

"The handsome widower, you mean?"

"Yes."

"He called you!"

"Well, yes, but it's not what you think." Leslie explained what had transpired, including their conversation about Joy. "So, see?" she said when she'd finished, "It's hopeless."

"What's hopeless?"

"Him. Can't you see it? He's so far from being ready for another relationship, there's no sense in me even thinking about it."

"Aha, so you *have* been thinking about it."

"You know I have."

"Well, yes, I do, because you wouldn't be talking about him so much if you hadn't. But I don't agree with you that it's a hopeless case. Just the fact that he's confided in you should tell you differently. He may not realize it yet, but he's interested in you, sweetie."

Hope flared, even as Leslie told herself it was silly to feel encouraged by Sandi's words. After all, Sandi was her friend. Her *best* friend. Of course, she would be loyal. Suddenly she felt foolish. What had she been thinking of, calling Sandi?

Leslie sighed. "No, Sandi," she said sadly. "I don't think so. I was just a comfortable shoulder, someone safe that he could talk to. And if he is attracted to me, it's probably because I remind him of his wife, not because of me personally. As much as I like him, I'm not sure I could handle that. I'm glad I told you, though, because talking about it has clarified the situation for me. I really think the wisest course would be for me to forget about him.''

The following morning, Leslie tried not to think about Brian coming at eleven, but she found herself watching the clock, anyway. At ten minutes before the hour, she went into the ladies' room and freshened her makeup and hair. It was only when she started to spritz herself with more perfume, that she stopped, telling herself enough was enough. Brian wasn't coming to the office to see her. Plus, hadn't she already decided he wasn't for her?

But no matter what she told herself, she couldn't seem to control her emotions, and her heart skipped crazily when Brian walked into the office a few minutes later. With superhuman effort, Leslie managed to conceal how glad she was to see him, and gave him the same composed greeting and friendly but casual smile she would give anyone.

Once again, he wore jeans—Leslie figured jeans were his standard attire at work—topped by a snug-fitting blue T-shirt the exact shade of his eyes.

''I'll let Dr. Singer know you're here,'' she said. Why did he have to look so good? Why couldn't he be homely and unattractive instead of so downright sexy?

''Okay.'' He smiled, and his eyes crinkled at the corners.

Leslie quickly walked back to Dr. Singer's office, even though she could have just buzzed him on the intercom. The doctor's door was open, and he was seated at his desk, reading a file.

"Dr. Singer?"

He looked up.

"Brian Canfield is here."

Dr. Singer smiled. "Send him in."

By the time Leslie returned to the outer office, she felt more in control. She escorted Brian back to Dr. Singer's office, and once the door shut behind him, she lectured herself sternly.

Later, as she sat at her desk and wondered what would be the outcome of the conversation going on between Brian and Dr. Singer, she sadly admitted that if Brian *did* decide to switch Jeffrey to a different therapist, for her anyway, it would probably be the best decision.

Brian was dismayed by the quick leap of pleasure he felt when he saw Leslie. She looked particularly attractive today, he thought, in a black-and-white striped blouse and a black skirt that stopped a few inches above the knees and showed off her long legs to advantage.

Jeffrey wasn't the only one with a problem, he thought as he followed Leslie into Dr. Singer's office.

"Well, Mr. Canfield, it's good to see you again," Dr. Singer said, rising and extending his hand.

Brian gripped it firmly. Although he'd only talked

with Dr. Singer once in person and a couple of times by telephone, he respected and liked the older man.

"So what can I do for you today?" the doctor asked once they were both seated, his eyes kind as they studied Brian.

Brian had given some thought to how to begin. "I know that the things Jeffrey tells you are confidential, Dr. Singer, but I was wondering...has he ever mentioned Leslie?"

Dr. Singer frowned. "Leslie? My Leslie?"

"Yes."

"I'm not sure I understand. In what context?"

"In relation to his mother."

Now Dr. Singer looked completely baffled. "No," he said slowly. "What possible connection could Leslie have to his mother?"

So Brian explained. He told the doctor about the way Leslie had affected him the first time he'd seen her and how he'd immediately seen the similarities between her and Joy. He also explained how attached to Leslie Jeffrey was.

"He talks about her all the time. I didn't really think that much of it at first, even though it is pretty unusual for an eleven-year-old boy to become so attached to an adult, especially so quickly. But once I'd met her, well, it was obvious to me why it had happened."

Dr. Singer rubbed his chin thoughtfully. "And now you're worried that Jeffrey's feelings for Leslie might be harmful to him."

"Yes," Brian said, relieved that Dr. Singer understood without Brian having to explain.

Dr. Singer sat quietly thinking for several long minutes. Then he sighed. "I understand why you're worried, and I agree that there might be some cause for concern. However, whatever harm there might be in this relationship, it has already been done."

Brian nodded.

"As I see it, the thing we must decide now is how to avoid doing even more harm to the boy." Again, Dr. Singer stroked his chin.

"I've considered switching him to another therapist," Brian said, deciding the situation called for frankness and total honesty.

"I can see why you might, but I don't think that's a good idea. Jeffrey and I have finally reached a point where he trusts me. Switching him to someone else could erase all the headway we've made. In addition, I think it is potentially more harmful to abruptly terminate his association with Leslie than it would be to continue it."

"So you think I should do nothing?"

"Why not give Jeffrey some time? He's a smart kid. He knows Leslie isn't his mother. Besides, his contact with her is quite limited. And it will come to a natural end when Jeffrey's therapy is concluded, by which time he will be emotionally stronger and better equipped to handle it."

"Trouble is," Brian said, "he's been pestering me lately to include her in outings with us." He explained how Jeffrey had finagled for Leslie to accompany them to the pizza parlor on Friday night and how he was now badgering Brian to invite her to Astroworld this coming weekend.

"Ahh, I see."

Belatedly, Brian wondered if he might be causing trouble for Leslie by telling Dr. Singer this. Was there some rule against fraternizing with the patients? "I don't want you to blame Leslie. Jeffrey really gave neither of us any choice. It's just I'm not sure what to do," he finished lamely.

"Does it make *you* uncomfortable to be around Leslie?"

"No, of course not." It was only *afterwards* that he felt uncomfortable, when he found himself spending far too much time thinking about her.

"Then my advice would be to treat the whole affair as naturally as possible," Dr. Singer said. "If you want to ask Leslie to accompany you and Jeffrey on an occasional outing, then by all means, do so. In fact, having her around in a normal setting might make Jeffrey realize more quickly that she's quite a different person than his mother, and he might get over his infatuation with her."

"Do you really think so?"

"Yes, I do. Demystifying her will probably work better than whatever idealized picture of her Jeffrey now has. In the meantime, I will talk to Jeffrey about her."

"Okay. Good."

"Don't worry, Mr. Canfield. We'll work this out."

"Thank you, Doctor." Brian wished he could unburden himself completely and tell Dr. Singer about his *own* confused feelings regarding Leslie, not to mention the way his in-laws might feel if they ever found out about her, but he knew he couldn't. Dr. Singer wasn't his doctor, he was Jeffrey's. If Brian needed help, he needed to find his own therapist. So he thanked the doctor and got up to leave.

"Keep me informed," Dr. Singer said. "Especially if anything else develops or the situation changes in any way."

"I will."

Brian walked out slowly. He felt relieved on the one hand; he would have hated having to tell Jeffrey he would no longer be seeing Dr. Singer. But on the other hand, he knew he still had a situation loaded with dynamite. And he would have to be very careful not to do anything that would set it off.

Normally Leslie looked forward to Tuesday nights when her glee club practiced. She sang alto in the four-part chorus, and no matter how stressful the day had been or how wound up or tired she might feel, singing with the group always relaxed her and made her feel good.

Unlike many of the other members of the group, Leslie was not well-grounded in music. She'd had a couple of years of piano lessons because her mother had insisted on it, but the piano had not been her forte, and even Peggy, as stubborn as she was, finally had to admit it and allow Leslie to quit. So although Leslie could sight-read music well enough to have passed the audition for the chorus, she had to concentrate fairly hard to be able to keep up with most of the others in her section.

That particular Tuesday night, she was having trouble concentrating. Images of Brian kept intruding. She was absurdly glad Dr. Singer had advised against Jeffrey switching therapists, even though she knew it would probably have been easier for her in the long run if her association with the Canfields was terminated now.

Finally the director dismissed them, and Leslie started gathering up her music.

"What's wrong, Leslie? Something bothering you tonight?"

Leslie turned to the woman who sat on her left. Mary Finnerty had become a good friend in the three years since Leslie had been associated with the group. "I'm sorry. I've been thinking about one of Dr. Singer's patients."

Mary's soft green eyes were sympathetic. "You're going to have to learn not to take your job home with you."

Leslie forced a lightness to her voice that she didn't feel. "Look who's talking."

Mary chuckled a bit sheepishly. She was a human resources manager for a large chemical company and an admitted workaholic. "Well, that's going to change."

"I've heard that before."

"This time I mean it. Look." Mary held out her left hand.

A large round diamond solitaire graced Mary's ring finger. Leslie blinked, and looked up, amazed. She'd known Mary was dating someone but had no idea it was serious. "When did *this* happen?"

"Last night."

Mary's face was rosy with happiness, something Leslie might have noticed if she hadn't been so wrapped up in herself all night, she thought guiltily.

"Oh, Mary, I'm so happy for you."

The two women hugged, and as they gathered their music and put it away, then walked outside to the parking lot and their respective cars, Mary gave Leslie a rundown on when, where, and how.

"My mother is over the moon," Mary said when she'd finished.

"I'll bet." Leslie and Mary had compared notes on their mothers for a long time. Like Leslie's, Mary's mother was obsessed with her daughter marrying and had just about given up on it ever happening, because Mary was forty-two years old and fiercely independent.

"And you know what?" Mary said. "I'm pretty thrilled myself. It's a funny thing. All these years I've made secret fun of women who didn't feel fulfilled unless they had a man, but now I understand, because without knowing I was ever missing anything, now I feel a completeness I never felt before."

Much later, lying in her bed upstairs, listening to

the wind rattle the leaves of the big aspen tree outside her window, Leslie thought about Mary's admission. She also thought about the shining happiness in her eyes and the softness in her voice.

That night she dreamed of Brian. In her dream he
was holding a ring. A diamond ring. It was her ring,
or at least she thought it was her ring. But when she
tried to take it, he closed his fist around it and said
she wasn't Joy and she'd never be Joy and she
couldn't have the ring. So saying, he turned and began to walk away. She ran after him, but the faster
she ran, the faster he walked, and no matter how she
tried, she couldn't catch up.

Brian let Jeffrey invite a friend over on Tuesday
afternoon, and that night he took them both out for
hamburgers and a movie. So when the friend's
mother invited Jeffrey to spend the night, Brian was
glad. He had a meeting with his accountant on
Thursday and needed to spend some time working
on the books. Not having to worry about entertain-
ing Jeffrey would free up that time.

All morning Wednesday, he and Brenda worked
on accounts. But Brian found it hard to concentrate
because images of Leslie kept intruding. Finally
Brenda noticed.

"Hey, boss man, what's up?" she said.

"Hmm?"

"Don't *hmm* me. I've known you for ten years.
Something's on your mind."

Brian smiled ruefully. He should have known he couldn't hide anything from Brenda.

"Come on, spill it," she said, grinning at him.

So he told her everything. And it felt good to tell her. So good he almost told her how attracted to Leslie he was and how that attraction made him feel guilty. But he stopped short of being *that* candid. It would be different if he intended to act on his inappropriate feelings for her, but he didn't.

"Yep. You've got a problem," Brenda said when he finished. "So what have you decided? You gonna invite her to go to Astroworld with you?"

"Despite what Dr. Singer said about demystifying her, I still think it would be best if I limit Jeffrey's contact with her. No, I'm not going to invite her to go, no matter how Jeffrey wheedles."

Brenda nodded, but the expression in her eyes was thoughtful, and Brian wondered what was going on in that shrewd head of hers. "You haven't told me what *you* think of the woman," she finally said.

"Me? I don't know. She's nice." He shrugged. "I liked her."

"Just nice?"

Brian smiled ruefully. "All right. She's very nice."

"Is she *really* like Joy?"

Brian considered the question. "Not really. But there *is* something…"

"I see." She sighed. "Well, I think you've made the right decision."

"Do you?"

"Yes. And not just for Jeffrey's sake."

"What do you mean?"

Now she smiled, but it was a kind smile, and her eyes had softened. She touched his hand. "You know, Brian, you're terribly vulnerable yourself. And it sounds to me as if being around this woman might be just as harmful to your well-being as it is to Jeffrey's. Because she's not Joy, and no amount of wishing on *your* part is going to change that."

Chapter Six

Wednesday night, on the way home from work, Brian stopped at the supermarket. They'd run out of milk and coffee, plus he was in the mood for ice cream. He stood at the freezer case, trying to decide between the merits of chocolate fudge and butter pecan and had almost decided to take a gallon of each when a familiar voice called, "Brian! Hi!"

He turned around, and sure enough, there stood a smiling Carole Sherman, who had been Joy's best friend all of her life. He hadn't seen Carole in months.

"Carole." He put his arms around her and gave her a hug. "It's great to see you."

"It's great to see you, too. How have you been?" Her eyes, filled with that combination of pity and concern he'd become accustomed to seeing, searched his face.

"Good," he said. "Good."

But he didn't meet her eyes, because seeing her brought back vivid memories of all the Friday nights he and Joy and Carole and her husband Johnny had spent together—going to movies and out to dinner or just visiting at each other's homes, playing games or cards. He was suddenly overwhelmed by one of those piercing feelings of loss that had come so often in the first months after Joy's death and only appeared occasionally now. And he knew, when he finally looked up, that Carole knew exactly what he was feeling.

"God, I miss her," she said huskily, her eyes filling.

Brian fought to control his own emotions.

"How's Jeffy doing?" she said after a moment. She had gained control of herself and her voice was determinedly cheery.

Brian smiled. "Much better."

"I'm glad. He's such a good kid. Johnny and I were just talking about him the other day. I can't remember now what it was, but something reminded us of that time when we were at your house. Maybe it was the Fourth of July. Anyway, we grilling some steaks in the backyard and he was playing and all of a sudden he climbed to the top of his sliding board—you remember, don't you?—he had gotten that Superman outfit for his birthday, I think it was his fifth, and he stood at the top of the steps and jumped 'cause he thought he could fly.''

Brian laughed, although at the time, all four of them—he and Joy, Carole and Johnny—had run to Jeffrey's side, afraid he'd broken some bones. But he'd looked up at them and grinned, so obviously pleased with himself, Brian hadn't the heart to do more than caution him against trying anything that dangerous again. "Yeah, I remember."

"I miss you and Jeffy, too," she said softly, squeezing his forearm. "Let's get together for dinner or something soon. Okay?"

"Sure."

"I mean it. I'm going to call you tonight, and we'll decide on a day."

He nodded.

They hugged again, and she left. Brian watched her walk away and thought about how different his life was now than it had been when Joy was alive. Joy had been a social person, and she loved having people over, loved going out. They'd not only spent their Friday nights with Carole and Johnny but had had a wide circle of friends and activities. Joy had been an opera buff, and for several years, they'd had season tickets to the Houston Grand Opera. She'd loved the theater, too, as well as any kind of live performance, so they'd seen practically every show at the Galveston Opera House and the Strand Street Theater.

Now Brian's social life consisted of kid movies and watching TV and once in a while, when Jeffrey was spending Saturday or Sunday with his grand-parents, he would get in a round of golf. Other than that, since Joy's death, Brian had reverted to type, refusing most invitations and sticking close to home.

It's not good for you, old man. It's not good for Jeffrey, either.

Pensive now, Brian put his ice cream in his basket and headed for the checkout lines. And as he did, he resolved to change. From now on, he would make an effort to see old friends and to try to make his and Jeffrey's life as close to what it was when Joy was alive as possible.

On Wednesday night Leslie went to the children's shelter where she'd been a volunteer for the past four years. Sometimes she thought about quitting because the work could be depressing, but the children were so deserving and needy, and many of them were so lovable, that every time she considered bailing out, she knew she never would.

Many of them came from abusive situations or had been abandoned by their single mothers. Most were earmarked for foster care and the shelter was just a temporary haven.

As she had many times before, Leslie wondered how anyone could abuse a helpless child. That night, as she bathed a ten-month-old baby whose back and buttocks bore faded bruises from an earlier beating, she thought about the kind of home life she could give a child, how she would cherish it and care for it and love it.

She lifted the little boy out of the tub and swaddled him in a big towel. While she was drying him, Judith Freeman, the director of the center, looked in on her. "How's he doing?" she said.

Leslie smiled. "He seemed to enjoy his bath." She cuddled the toddler. "Didn't you, Michael?"

The trusting smile he gave her tugged at her heart. She kissed his forehead. "He's such a sweetheart."

"Yes," Judith said. "He is."

"What's the story? Is he going into foster care?" The shelter was a temporary solution for these children. Those who couldn't go home again would go into the foster care system. Some would eventually go back to their homes; others would be adopted.

Judith nodded. "The father is long gone, and the mother's been arrested for dealing."

"Was she the one who abused him?"

"We think it was her boyfriend."

Leslie sighed. Same old story, just different players.

By the time she said her goodbyes and headed for home, she had made a decision. No more mooning over Brian Canfield and his son. She had gotten along fine before they came along, and she would get along fine after they were gone.

What she *did* need and want, though, was a child of her own, and to that end, she would begin her investigation into the possibilities of adoption first thing tomorrow morning.

"My earliest available appointment is next Wednesday. Could you make it at two o'clock?"

"Is it possible to come earlier? I'm free between noon and two," Leslie said. If she *had* to take time off to see the woman at the adoption agency, she would, but it would make it so much easier if they could work around Leslie's schedule.

"No, Miss Marlowe, I'm sorry. We're very busy, you know," the counselor said with a trace of annoyance coloring her tone.

"Two o'clock will be fine," Leslie said hurriedly. She certainly didn't want to prejudice the woman against her before she'd even been interviewed.

"Good. We'll see you then."

Leslie let out a gust of breath as she replaced the receiver. She'd taken the first step. A combination of anticipation and fear caused flutters in her stomach. What if the counselor didn't like her? What if she didn't make a good impression?

Now stop that, she told herself. *You have nothing to fear. Just go to the agency, be sincere and honest, and let the rest take care of itself.*

There were plenty of single women adopting babies, and there was no reason for her not to be one of them. After all, she was young and healthy, had a good job, a nice home that she owned free and clear, and she had a stable history. Not only that, she worked with children and knew about children. Surely that would count for a lot.

Who knew? She might even get a baby.

On that happy thought, she turned her attention back to her work and was soon immersed.

* * *

Brian brought Jeffrey to the office with him on Thursday, where Brenda put him to work on a customer mailing. Brian was amused and a bit touched to see how diligently Jeffrey applied himself to the task and how much pleasure he derived from it.

At eleven, Brian met with his accountant, and afterwards, he and Jeffrey took off and went to lunch, followed by a movie. On the way home they stopped to pick up some chicken and coleslaw.

After dinner, Jeffrey helped clear the table without being asked, and Brian geared himself for what he was sure was coming. Sure enough, a few minutes later, Jeffrey said, "Are we gonna ask Leslie to go with us on Saturday, Dad?"

"No, Jeffrey, I don't think so. But if you want to invite one of your friends, that's fine with me."

"But Dad…Leslie *is* my friend, and she's the one I want to ask."

Brian sighed. "Look, son, I know you want her, but I don't think it's a good idea."

"Why not?" Jeffrey's expression was mutinous.

What could he say? "I really can't explain it. I just don't think it's a good idea. Now can we leave it at that?" Brian felt bad about using that tone with Jeffrey, but he could see if he wasn't firm, Jeffrey would just keep on badgering him until he gave in.

Jeffrey lapsed into a sullen silence that was unlike him, and no matter what Brian said to try to lighten the atmosphere, Jeffrey didn't respond.

Brian thought about introducing the subject again, then decided against it. Obviously Jeffrey had finally accepted that Brian wasn't going to change his mind, and even though he was mad at his father now, he would get over it.

So Brian said nothing. And as soon as the kitchen was cleaned up, Jeffrey mumbled that he was going to his room, and that was the last Brian saw of him until bedtime.

"You mad at me?" Brian asked as he went into Jeffrey's room to say good-night.

Jeffrey shrugged.

Brian waited, but nothing else was forthcoming. "Well, good night, then. See you in the morning."

The next morning—Friday—Jeffrey was back to his genial self, and Brian breathed a sigh of relief. He'd taken the day off, and they had invited Jeffrey's Sea World friend, Scott, to go with them to tour NASA.

They spent an enjoyable day at the space center and almost didn't make it back to Galveston in time for Jeffrey's four-o'clock appointment with Dr. Singer, but Brian managed to get him there with only minutes to spare.

"I'll take Scott home, then come back here to pick you up," he told Jeffrey.

"Okay, Dad, see you later."

Jeffrey liked going to see Dr. Singer. He could tell him anything, and Dr. Singer would listen. He wasn't like some adults, who pretended to listen, but never *really* heard what you said.

"It's good to see you, Jeffrey," Dr. Singer said when Jeffrey walked into his office.

Jeffrey smiled. "I just got back from NASA. Dad took me and Scott."

"Is Scott one of your friends?"

"Yep."

"Well, sit down and tell me about your week."

So Jeffrey did. When he was finished Dr. Singer said, "No problems? No bad dreams or anything?"

Jeffrey shook his head. "No, but…" He stopped, unsure how to say what he wanted to say.

"But…"

"I, uh…I did want to talk to you about something."

"All right."

"Do you think it's okay to pray to my mom?"

"*Have* you been praying to your mom?"

Jeffrey nodded.

"Well, Jeffrey, I don't see how there could be any harm in praying to your mom, especially if it makes you feel better."

Jeffrey let out a breath. "It does make me feel better."

Dr. Singer didn't say anything for a few minutes. He just looked at Jeffrey. Then, in that quiet way he had, he said, "I've noticed that you and Leslie have become friends."

Jeffrey smiled. "Yeah, she's nice."

"She certainly is."

Jeffrey waited, but Dr. Singer didn't say anything else, so he said, "My dad likes her, too."

"Does he?"

"Uh-huh. I asked him. You know what he said?"

"No, what did he say?"

"He said Leslie was kinda like my mom."

"Do *you* think she's like your mom?"

"Well, I didn't, but after he said that, I kinda do."

"Do you suppose that's why you like her so much? Because she's kind of like your mom?"

Jeffrey shrugged. "I don't know. Maybe."

"She's not your mom, though."

"I know."

Dr. Singer was quiet for a long time. When he spoke, his voice was soft. "What is it about Leslie that you like the best?"

Jeffrey thought about the question for a few moments before answering. "She makes me feel good when I'm with her, because she listens to me and she doesn't treat me like a little kid. And she doesn't feel *sorry* for me. Ever since my mom died, all these people feel *sorry* for me. I hate that."

Dr. Singer studied him thoughtfully. "You sound as if you're really thinking straight these days, Jeffrey."

Jeffrey beamed at the unexpected praise. He couldn't wait to tell his dad, 'cause he knew his dad worried about him, but if Dr. Singer thought he was thinking straight, that meant he was almost well.

His dad was gonna be *so* happy.

Maybe now he'd even let Jeffrey invite Leslie to go to Astroworld tomorrow.

* * *

Once Brian had deposited Scott safely at his home, he had about thirty minutes to kill before having to pick Jeffrey up, and he fully intended to spend them at the hardware store or someplace similar, but instead found himself in the parking lot of Dr. Singer's building.

He told himself the only reason he was there early was to ensure that Jeffrey didn't take matters into his own hands and invite Leslie to Astroworld himself.

But when Brian walked into Dr. Singer's office and Leslie's desk was clean and her chair empty, he couldn't deny the disappointment he felt. He finally admitted to himself that he'd wanted to see her. He also knew it was a good thing she wasn't there today, because the emotions she produced in him were ones he was ill-equipped to deal with.

He sat down and listlessly picked up a copy of *National Geographic*. A few minutes later, the inner door opened and Leslie, looking far more attractive in a slim-fitting green dress than any woman had a right to look, walked out.

"Oh!" she said, cheeks coloring. "I—I didn't know you were here."

Brian stood, the magazine falling to the floor. When he grabbed for it, he cracked the back of his knuckles on the coffee table. He winced, feeling like an idiot. "I just got here a minute ago."

For the space of seconds that seemed much longer, they stood there, looking at each other and saying nothing. The silence stretched. Finally, she seemed to give herself a little shake. "Um, do you want some coffee?"

"I don't think so, but thanks."

She nodded and walked to her desk.

Brian sat down again. So did she. Her hair, which was normally held back from her face by combs, hung loose today, and it curled softly around her chin.

She was a lovely woman, he thought. Not the kind that struck you as beautiful, but the kind that grew on you, so that each time you saw her you thought she was more attractive than the time before.

As he watched, she opened a drawer of her desk, removed a folder, then turned toward her computer and began to type.

Brian was still holding the magazine, and he opened it. There was a story about Australia in this issue, and he turned pages until he found it. He stared at the photograph of an Aborigine, seeing it, yet not seeing it.

The minutes ticked away. He heard the sounds of paper shuffling, the squeak of her chair, the click of computer keys.

Unable to resist, he glanced her way again. Just as he did, she turned, and their eyes connected. Then she quickly turned back to her work, and Brian's gaze returned to the magazine. This time, he forced himself to read.

At five o'clock, Jeffrey emerged.

Leslie turned at the sound, and Brian replaced the magazine on the coffee table and stood.

"Ready to go?" he said, smiling at Jeffrey.

"I guess so," said Jeffrey, although he sounded uncertain. He looked at Brian, then at Leslie.

"Goodbye, Jeffrey," she said, giving him a warm smile. "Have a good weekend."

Jeffrey dug the toe of his sneaker into the carpet. "We're goin' to Astroworld tomorrow."

"That should be a lot of fun."

"Yeah. Gee," he added wistfully, "I wish you were goin' with us." He avoided Brian's eyes. "Have you ever been there? It's really neat. You'd like it. Especially the roller coasters! They're my favorite." He finally looked up at Brian. "Wouldn't she like it, Dad?"

Brian rarely got angry with Jeffrey, but right now he could have cheerfully throttled him. "She'd probably like it about as much as I do," he said dryly, giving her one of those we-adults-must-stick-together looks.

If Jeffrey understood Brian's lame attempt at humor, he pretended he didn't. Instead, he smiled happily, saying, "See? Dad thinks you'd like it. Why don't you come with us, Leslie? It'll be a lot of fun."

Brian couldn't believe it. He had expressly told Jeffrey he did not intend to invite Leslie to go with them, and Jeffrey was blatantly defying him. When he got Jeffrey alone, he was going to give him a talking-to he would never forget. He felt like yanking him outside this very minute, but of course, he couldn't. He looked at Leslie.

Her brown eyes met his. Her cheeks were too pink, and he knew that once again, his son had managed to put him in an impossible position.

Brian knew when he was beaten. "Why *don't* you come with us?"

She shook her head. "Thank you. It's nice of you to ask, but I can't."

"Please," Jeffrey said.

Brian knew she was embarrassed. He also knew he had to do something to make things right. "As you can see, it means a lot to Jeffrey." Suddenly, he realized he wanted her to come. Very much. "And it would mean a lot to me, too," he added honestly.

For a moment, he was certain she'd refuse.

But finally, she said, "Are you sure?"

He smiled and nodded, the doubts that had plagued him for days gone as if they'd never existed. "I'm sure."

Now she smiled, too. "In that case, I'd love to go."

As Leslie drove home, she thought about what had happened and knew she had probably made a mistake in saying she'd accompany Brian and Jeffrey to Astroworld the next day. She liked Brian far too much, and when he had added his voice to Jeffrey's and encouraged her to go with them, she had been powerless to say no. The combination of father and son and the chance to spend an entire day in their company was simply irresistible.

. But it was stupid to have said yes. There was no future in it, and the more she was with them, the harder it was going to be to face that fact.

You're setting yourself up to get hurt. Really hurt.

Maybe she should call Brian and tell him she couldn't go, after all. That was the sensible thing to do.

But she knew she wasn't going to. She was going to take a chance. If she ended up getting hurt, well, so be it. She would survive.

She remembered a conversation she'd had with her grandmother shortly before she died. Nana was sitting propped up in her bed, Leslie in a chair beside her, and they'd been looking through old photo albums, while her grandmother had reminisced about her grandfather and how they'd met.

"Here we are on our wedding day," she said, pointing to a black-and-white snapshot of two attractive young people dressed in their wedding finery.

Leslie's eyes got misty every time she saw the photograph. "Grandfather was so handsome," she said softly.

"Yes," her grandmother said. "A handsome devil, that's what my mother said the first time she met him."

There were other photographs. One of Leslie's grandparents with a newborn Peggy. Another of her grandfather at the beach, arms around her grandmother, who was laughing. They both looked impossibly young.

And then, on the next page, a five-by-seven-inch photo of Leslie's grandfather in his U.S. Navy uniform.

With tears sparking her eyes, Leslie's grandmother talked about how much it had hurt when he'd died.

"When that telegram came, I didn't want to believe it. We'd only been married four years. And your mother was only three years old."

Leslie's Grandfather Ridgeway had died in World War II; his plane had gone down off the coast of Corregidor.

"But you know," her grandmother continued softly, "the hurt was worth it, because at least we'd had those four years together." She clasped Leslie's hand. "Remember that, my dear, and don't be afraid to take chances in your life."

Leslie smiled at the bittersweet memory. Her grandmother had had courage. She had faced life bravely, unafraid of what the future held.

"Okay, Gran," Leslie said aloud. "You'd be proud of me. I'm going to follow your example. I'm going to Astroworld with Brian and Jeffrey tomorrow, and Wednesday I'm meeting with the adoption agency counselor."

If someone had asked Brian what made him urge Leslie to go with them tomorrow, he wouldn't be able to say. He certainly hadn't intended to do it. But he wasn't sorry. In fact, he was eagerly looking forward to spending the day in Leslie's company.

And who knew? Maybe Dr. Singer was right. Maybe after tomorrow Jeffrey would realize Leslie was really very different from his mother, and he would no longer obsess over her.

In fact, having her go with them was probably a smart move on Brian's part. Reverse psychology, wasn't that what this was called? He must have realized that all the time. That was probably why he'd asked her to go along.

Yeah, sure. Tell me another one.

Brian ignored the voice in his head that was trying to shoot holes in his justification. Right now, he simply didn't care. He was following some instinct that told him this was the right thing to do.

Chapter Seven

Leslie awakened at five o'clock on Saturday morning, and no matter how she tried to get back to sleep, she couldn't. Finally, when her bedside clock read a quarter of six, she gave up.

Rising, she carefully stepped over Amber, who, as usual, had parked her overweight self right next to Leslie's bed.

"Lazy thing," Leslie said affectionately, reaching down to scratch the dog's head. She'd had the golden retriever almost eleven years. She had gotten her less than two weeks after the divorce. It had been her first act of independence, because throughout the years of her marriage, Elliott had refused to allow her to have a pet.

"Pets make messes, and I don't like messes,"

he'd said when she'd asked about getting a puppy or a kitten.

That was an understatement, Leslie had soon realized. Elliott not only didn't like messes, he expected everything in his life to be perfect. Her, the clothes she wore, the food she cooked, their home, their yard, their cars. And without exception, that perfection was her responsibility. The few times she'd asked for his help, he'd said, with exaggerated patience, as if she were a child, that it was her job to take care of all these details. After all, what else did she have to do?

She had wanted to work. She'd been offered a part-time job at a small art gallery owned by a friend of her mother's. But he had firmly refused. "The small amount of money you would earn would not be worth it," he'd said, giving her one of his condescending looks. "There's plenty to keep you busy here." She knew it would be useless to explain that working at the gallery would give her a chance to be with people and gain self-confidence.

So she'd stayed at home and tried to be the wife that Elliott expected. She took courses in flower arranging and gourmet cooking, because Elliott made it very clear that meals of macaroni and cheese or meat loaf would not be tolerated. When he arrived home at six, he wanted a chilled martini—which she quickly learned to make—followed by dinner at precisely six-thirty on a beautifully set table. The only time his timetable varied was when he had a meeting that necessitated an earlier dinner hour.

He wanted an immaculate house: furniture shining with polish, crisp tablecloths, fresh flowers in sparkling vases, beds made to his exacting standards. And woe betide her if he found even a speck of soap to mar the shine of the bathroom faucets or one of the double sinks.

She still shuddered when she remembered the evening they'd entertained his boss and several co-workers and their wives. Leslie had slaved for days over the menu: stuffed mushrooms and miniquiches with cocktails, and a dinner that started with a clear soup, then a salad of Romaine lettuce over which she had drizzled a raspberry vinaigrette, followed by a standing rib roast, new potatoes in butter and chives, fresh asparagus with Hollandaise sauce, and a dessert of double-fudge brownies topped by real whipped cream.

Leslie was so nervous throughout the meal she could hardly eat. Everything had gone well; the guests were highly complimentary, and she knew Elliott was pleased. And then disaster struck. Just as Leslie was serving dessert, she saw a shadow out of the corner of her eye. Looking up, she discovered a giant cockroach on the chandelier—one of the tree roaches so common to south Texas. She'd started to shake. Elliott would blame her, even though it was hardly her fault a roach had managed to get inside their house. For several long, agonizing minutes, she tried to think what to do. Should she point the pesky insect out, make a joke of it, and get the men to get rid of it? Or should she simply pray no one would notice and the roach would eventually disappear?

While her mind whirled and her stomach churned, the unthinkable happened. The roach fell off the chandelier and landed right in the middle of the table. The women shrieked, several jumped up, one overturned her coffee cup and the liquid spilled over the front of her sequined dress. Bedlam followed, during which Elliott gave Leslie a malevolent look that told her she would suffer for a long time over this fiasco.

It took a long time for Leslie to realize that Elliott didn't love her, that in his eyes, she was simply there to serve. When she pleased him, he treated her well. When she didn't, after an initial ugly denunciation, he gave her the silent treatment.

After her second miscarriage, he didn't touch her for six months. He blamed her, and even though intellectually she knew better, she couldn't help wondering if, as Elliott implied, she *had* done something to bring about the miscarriage.

It was years before she stopped feeling guilty.

Her life was so different now.

She was so different now.

Now she had Amber, she had a job, and if she felt like eating her dinner at ten o'clock at night, she could. In fact, if she didn't feel like eating at all, she didn't have to. And her home was peaceful. Peaceful and calm. There was none of the underlying tension that had been so pervasive throughout all the years of her marriage.

Married to Elliott, she'd been so afraid she was going to do or say something wrong, or had *already* done or said something wrong, she could never relax. In fact, she'd ground her teeth so much the dentist had made a night guard for her.

But most of all, she now had confidence in herself and her abilities. Now she knew she was okay. More than okay. She was an attractive, intelligent, sensitive, caring human being. She didn't have to take a back seat to anyone.

Still thinking about the past, she put on her robe and headed for the bathroom. Ten minutes later, teeth brushed, hair combed, face washed, she headed downstairs.

She turned on the coffeemaker, and once it was ready, poured herself a mugful and carried it outside to the back porch. She slowly sipped while she watched the sun rise and listened to the birds chirping in the dozens of trees that dotted her backyard.

She loved this house. She had always loved it. Her fondest memories of childhood had been coming here to visit her grandmother, who had always had time to listen and had taught Leslie so much. Her grandmother had been an avid gardener, and she'd patiently shown Leslie how to care for the flowers and plants. Leslie, like all children, had loved digging in the dirt and "helping."

Since inheriting the house, Leslie had tried to keep up her grandmother's flower beds and garden, but working full time made it difficult, so last year she'd given in and hired a man to help. Robert came twice a week now, and the healthy-looking plants and flowers reflected the extra attention.

Leslie justified the expense by the fact that she didn't have a rent payment or a house payment like most people. Of course, she thought wryly, her taxes were high enough, and the insurance for the old house was astronomical. But she had gotten a decent settlement from Elliott. Even though her mother wasn't happy about it, Leslie's father had made sure she had a good lawyer representing her in the divorce. And since then, he'd helped her learn about investing her money, so it had grown, even though she'd used some of it a couple of times, once to replace her grandmother's antiquated appliances, and a couple of years ago to buy herself a new car.

As daylight crept over the horizon, her thoughts wandered, gradually moving to the upcoming day and how much she was looking forward to it.

She decided that, for today at least, she would enjoy being with Brian and Jeffrey, and she wouldn't worry about the future. Perhaps this would be the last time she'd spend in their company, and from now on her only contact with Jeffrey would be when he came to the office. *Fine,* she thought. *Whatever the future holds in that regard, I'll handle it. In the meantime, I'm going to make the most of today.*

By eight forty-five, Leslie was ready. She was dressed in comfortable khaki walking shorts and a cool white cotton blouse. She'd brushed her hair back and secured it with a headband. A small canvas tote held everything she'd need for the day.

Amber, who was smart enough to know her mistress was going somewhere, hung close. Leslie felt kind of bad about leaving the dog for the entire day, but she had plenty of food and water, and the back porch was shady and sheltered, so she would be fine.

"C'mon," Leslie said. "Time to go out."

The dog dug in her heels when Leslie tried to lead her to the back door.

"All right," Leslie said. "How about if I give you a treat?"

The bribe succeeded. Once the dog was on the porch eating her dog biscuit, Leslie locked the back door and walked out to the living room. Just as she did, she saw a black Suburban pulling into the driveway and a moment later, Brian getting out. He, too, wore khaki shorts, paired with a dark brown knit shirt. His legs were muscular and nicely shaped, as tanned as the rest of him. He either spent his free time at the beach or wore shorts at work, she decided, then chuckled. How silly she was. What difference did it make why he was tanned? All she knew was, she liked the way he looked.

Picking up her canvas tote, she walked outside, locking the door behind her.

"What a terrific house," Brian said, stopping on the driveway to study the green frame Victorian-era home. "Look at those cupolas. How'd it survive the Great Storm?"

He was referring to the fierce hurricane that

slammed Galveston Island in September 1900 and demolished countless homes and buildings. It had been an awful time in the city's history. More than six thousand people died, including several of Leslie's ancestors.

"It very nearly didn't," Leslie said, reaching his side. "About two-thirds of the house was destroyed. But my great-grandfather, with help from my uncle, rebuilt it the following summer."

"Looks like they did a great job. Maybe one of these days you'll give me a tour."

"I'd love to."

He eyed her tote. "You ready?"

"Yes."

He helped her into the truck, and that was the first she realized there was another youngster besides Jeffrey inside.

"Leslie, this is Mark Fabrizio, a friend of Jeffrey's. Mark, this is Leslie Marlowe."

A dark-haired boy with friendly brown eyes smiled at her. "Hi."

"Hello, Mark."

"We decided last night that it would be more fun for Jeffrey if he had someone along who actually enjoyed going on some of these rides," Brian explained as he pulled out of the driveway.

Leslie smiled. "Good thinking."

The drive from Galveston to Houston took about ninety minutes, so it was ten-thirty before they pulled into the Astroworld parking lot and nearly eleven before they gained admittance to the park.

Jeffrey and Mark immediately wanted to ride the Texas Cyclone, so they headed in that direction.

"You want to try this demon, too?" Brian asked when they reached the ride.

"Why not?" Leslie said. She hadn't ridden a roller coaster in years, but she was game.

The line was already long, but it moved fairly quickly. Jeffrey and Mark climbed into one seat, and Brian and Leslie sat behind them. As the ride started, Brian grinned at her and said, "Hang on tight."

After that, everything was a blur. The car moved so fast through the twists and turns that all Leslie could do was hang on and scream with the rest of the riders.

After it was over, the boys were exhilarated and wanted to ride the coaster again, but Brian and Leslie, practically in unison, said, "No way. Not me." Then they both laughed.

"I think we'll sit this one out," Brian said, "but you boys go on."

So they found a bench close by.

"Whew," Brian said, "I'm too old for rides like that."

Leslie grimaced. "Me, too." She actually hurt from the force of the ride. "I have a feeling I'm going to be sore tonight!"

They sat in companionable silence for a while. Leslie watched the people going by, paying particular attention to the families. They all looked so happy and carefree. She knew this was an illusion.

Most families had problems, and some would inevitably be serious ones. Even so, they had each other, and nothing seemed as bad when you had someone to share it with.

She glanced at Brian, who was sitting with his long legs extended out in front of him. She wondered what he was thinking.

As if he felt her eyes on him, he turned her way. "You thirsty?"

"A little. Are you?"

"Actually, I'm hungry, but that's because I only ate a piece of toast for breakfast. Think we could persuade those kids to stop for a while and let us eat some lunch?"

"Might be a hard sell," she said.

Sure enough, when the boys had finished their ride, they were less than enthusiastic about eating lunch right then, so Brian compromised. "You can ride two more rides, then we'll break for lunch, okay?"

Later, as they sat at a shaded table outside and ate their hamburgers and french fries, Leslie pretended they were a family. She told herself the pretense was innocent, and as long as neither Jeffrey nor Brian knew what was going on in her head, there was no harm done. But she knew she was fooling herself. The pretense *wasn't* innocent. It was dangerous, because it wasn't going to happen, and by continuing it and allowing herself to revel in it, she was setting herself up to be hurt in a big way.

But it didn't matter.

Nothing mattered except the knowledge that right now, there was nowhere else she'd rather be and no one else she'd rather be with.

It was early evening. They'd just finished eating dinner, and Jeffrey and Mark were riding the Sky-screamer for at least the eighth time that day. Leslie had gone in search of the ladies' rest room, and Brian stood a short distance from the ride and waited for the boys to finish and Leslie to rejoin him. He idly watched the people walking by.

Then suddenly, a short distance away, he spied Linette and Gerald Hadley walking toward him. Linette and Gerald were probably his in-laws' closest friends. They hadn't seen him; they were talking with a younger couple and were surrounded by several children. Brian recognized one of them as their grandson.

Just as he decided he'd rather not be seen, Linette looked in his direction. She smiled and waved, and Brian had no choice but to smile back.

"Well, Brian, how nice to see you. It's been such a long time," Linette said as they reached his side. Immediately, she must have remembered just when they *had* actually seen each other, and she became flustered, for it had been at Joy's funeral.

"Too long," Brian said easily, not wanting her to feel bad. He turned to shake hands with Gerald, then was introduced to the others: their daughter Emily and her husband, then their three grandchildren, but all the while his mind was churning. What if Leslie came back now? What would the Hadleys think? And what if they said something to the Paladinos?

He could hardly concentrate on what Linette was saying. Finally, he had to ask her to repeat her question.

"I said, is Jeffrey here?"

"Yeah, he's riding the Skyscreamer with his friend, Mark."

Gerald chuckled. "And you're sensibly *not* riding that monster."

Although the Hadley grandchildren were restlessly waiting to get going again, the elder Hadleys seemed in no hurry to leave. Brian tried not to look in the direction Leslie had gone, but he wanted to be forewarned if she did return, even though he had no idea what he would say about her. He could hardly explain that she was Jeffrey's friend. *Besides, that's not true anymore. She's your friend, too.*

But Leslie's return wasn't the only thing he had to worry about. The ride would probably be over at any moment, and Jeffrey and Mark would rejoin him. And if Leslie wasn't here, Jeffrey would be sure to ask where she'd gone. Then Brian would still have to explain her presence.

He thought his worrying was for nothing when Gerald Hadley said, "Well, these children are getting impatient, so I guess we'll be going. It was good seeing you, Brian." The others echoed his sentiments and said their goodbyes.

And just at that moment, Leslie walked up to

them. Linette looked at her, a puzzled expression on her face. Leslie smiled uncertainly.

Brian hoped his face didn't betray his dismay. He smiled and, turning to Leslie, said, "Leslie, I'd like you to meet some friends." He made the introductions, ending with, "And this is Leslie Marlowe, a friend of mine and Jeffrey's."

Linette's gray eyes reflected her surprise as she shook Leslie's hand. Gerald's merely seemed curious.

Brian hoped they wouldn't change their minds and linger, and they didn't. Linette said, "Nice meeting you, Leslie," which was echoed by her husband, and then they left.

Brian was ashamed of how upset he felt by the encounter, because Leslie was the kind of woman any man should be proud to be seen with. But his feelings had nothing to do with Leslie as a person. He just didn't want to upset Hank and Theresa, and they *would* be upset when Linette told them about seeing him here with Leslie. They would think he was dating her, and it wasn't like that at all.

But maybe Linette wouldn't say anything. Maybe by the time Hank and Theresa returned from Canada, Linette would have forgotten all about today.

He hoped so. Because if and when he began seeing a woman again, he needed to prepare the Paladinos. He couldn't just spring someone on them. He would need to tell them before the fact. Let them know he was thinking about dating, so they wouldn't be shocked when it happened.

Suddenly he realized that he'd spent nearly an entire day without thinking about Joy once. If he hadn't run into the Hadleys, he might not have thought of her at all. Guilt suffused him, and try as he might, he couldn't banish it.

All at once, he was ready to go home. "Well, what do you guys think?" He looked at the boys. "Ready to call it a day?"

"No, Dad!" exclaimed Jeffrey. "It's still early."

"It's seven-thirty," Brian pointed out. "We've been here nearly nine hours, and we've got a good hour and a half drive ahead of us. Hey, I know you kids never wear out, but I'm beat." He looked at Leslie. "I'll bet you are, too."

"I am a little tired," she admitted, giving Jeffrey an apologetic smile.

"Aw, Dad...can't we stay just a little while longer? We wanna ride the Dungeon Drop and Greased Lightning again."

Mark didn't say anything, but his expression said it for him.

"Oh, all right," Brian said. "Another half hour. But that's *it,* Jeffrey."

"Okay, Dad, thanks!"

So for the next thirty minutes the boys rode their favorite rides, and Brian and Leslie found a place to sit and wait.

"It's been such a nice day," Leslie said. "Thank you for asking me to come along."

"I'm glad you did. Otherwise, I'd have been

forced to sit by myself or worse.'' He gave a mock shudder. ''I'd have to ride with those kids.''

''They're amazing, aren't they? They never get tired.''

''Yeah. I remember when Jeffrey was a toddler. I used to watch him and wish I had half his energy.''

''I'll bet he was cute as a toddler.''

''We thought he was the best-looking kid in the universe.''

She smiled, but there was a tinge of sadness in her expression. Leaning forward, she rested her elbows on her knees, and without looking at him, said, ''I have an appointment with an adoption agency next week.''

She'd startled him, and it was a moment before he replied. ''You thinking about adopting a child?''

She turned to face him. The evening sun fired her hair from behind with a halo of gold, and for just an instant, he was struck with a strange sense of déjà vu. ''Yes,'' she said softly. ''Do you think that's crazy?''

''You mean because you're single?''

She nodded. ''Yes.''

''Lots of people are raising children on their own. Hell, *I* am.''

''It's not easy, though, is it?''

''No, it's not easy.''

She sighed deeply and looked away again. ''I want a child so badly.''

For the first time since meeting her, Brian stopped thinking of her in relation to himself or Jeffrey, and started thinking of her in terms of who *she* was. "Then I think it's great you're considering adopting." He realized he knew very little about her. During the times they'd spent together, he'd done most of the talking. And when she *did* talk, it was about Jeffrey or him, never about herself. Now he found himself very curious. Had she ever been in love? Married? And if not, why not?

As if she'd read his mind, she said, "I was married for five years."

Brian waited.

"We both wanted children, but I..." She swallowed. "It turns out I couldn't have any." There was a catch in her voice.

Because he didn't know what to say, he simply reached over and squeezed her forearm.

When she finally turned to look at him, her eyes were bright. "I'm sorry."

"Nothing to be sorry for."

It was probably a good thing the boys came up just then, because their presence diffused the emotional moment. But as they prepared to leave and for a long time after, Brian thought about what she'd said. He wasn't sure any man could ever really understand the pain a woman felt when she wanted children and wasn't able to have them, but he thought he had a pretty good idea of what she'd suffered, because he remembered how disappointed he and Joy had been when they'd thought they couldn't have more children, and they already had one.

He tried to imagine life without Jeffrey.

No one to fill the house with noise. No one to laugh with or cry with. No one to hug at bedtime. No one to love.

Brian realized he had a lot to be thankful for.

Brian was too quiet on the way home. Leslie was sure she knew why and she mentally kicked herself for having said what she did about not being able to have children. Too late she remembered what he'd told her about Joy's being pregnant when she was killed.

You are so stupid! she chided herself.

Thank goodness for the boys. They filled the car with their chatter and laughter all the way home.

By the time they crossed the causeway bridge onto the island, full night had fallen, and the waters of the bay shimmered in the moonlight. Leslie stared out the window pensively.

"Do you mind if I drop Mark at home first?"

Leslie jumped. Brian was talking to her, she realized. "No, of course not."

Mark lived at the other end of the island from Brian and Jeffrey, and Leslie wondered how the two boys had become friends. "They used to be in the same Scout troop," Brian explained. "Before Mark moved."

After dropping Mark, Brian headed toward Leslie's house.

"Thank you again for a lovely day," she said when he pulled into her driveway.

"I'm glad you went with us," he said. "I had a good time, and I know Jeffrey did, too."

"Yeah," Jeffrey echoed. "It was great!"

An awkward silence fell between them. Leslie hoped Brian would say something about seeing her again, but it didn't look as if he was going to, and disappointment settled in her chest like a dead weight.

Before she could give it too much thought and perhaps lose her nerve, she said, "Turnabout is fair play, so in return for such a great day, how about you guys coming over for dinner tomorrow night? I make the best spaghetti sauce and meatballs you've ever tasted."

"Cool," Jeffrey said eagerly. "Spaghetti's my favorite."

"You don't have to do that," Brian said.

"I want to. Besides, you wanted to see my house, and daytime is best. Why don't you and Jeffrey come about five? We'll eat early, since Monday's a work day. You don't already have plans, do you?" She was talking too fast, but she couldn't seem to stop herself.

"No..."

"We never have any plans," Jeffrey said. "Do we, Dad?"

Brian laughed and shook his head. "I guess that settles it. We'll see you tomorrow."

Just what did he think he was doing? Brian asked himself as he drove home. How, in the space of two days, had he gone from the decision that he wouldn't spend any additional time with Leslie outside of Dr. Singer's office to spending not only all day today with her, but promising to spend tomorrow evening at her home?

This is a mistake.

Well, maybe it was, yet what could he have done differently? Since a week ago, when he'd first laid eyes on her, his entire life seemed to be spinning out of his control.

Trouble was, he liked spending time with her. Today had been one of the best and most enjoyable days he'd had since Joy's death. Leslie was easy to be with. He felt comfortable with her in a way he had never expected to feel with any woman again.

Suddenly, he knew if he let himself he could fall in love with Leslie. The knowledge shook him. He wanted to deny it, but he knew it was true, and if he denied it, he'd only be lying to himself.

I'm not ready.

It's too soon.

He remembered the stricken faces of Hank and Theresa as they said their final goodbyes to their beloved daughter.

They need more time, too.

That realization, more than any other, gave him new resolve. No matter how tempting, tomorrow *had* to be the last time he spent in Leslie's company.

Chapter Eight

Although it was ten o'clock and close to her parents' bedtime, Leslie thought she'd better tell her mother tonight that she wasn't going to make the family dinner tomorrow afternoon.

Sure enough, her parents had already retired for the night, and her mother's voice sounded cross when she answered the phone.

"Mom, I'm sorry. I know you were probably already in bed, but I just got home, and I wanted to let you know I won't be there for dinner tomorrow afternoon."

"Oh? Why not?"

Leslie told herself not to get angry. "Because I have other plans."

"Who is it, Peg?" sounded her father's mumbled voice in the background.

"It's Leslie."

"Something wrong?"

Leslie could picture her parents in their big double bed, her father blinking without his glasses, her mother frowning over at him.

"Nothing's wrong," her mother snapped. "Go back to sleep."

Leslie sighed. Maybe she should have just called in the morning, while they were at church, and left a message on their recorder.

"Did you forget we're celebrating Nicky's birthday tomorrow?" her mother said.

Oh, no. She *had* forgotten her nephew's thirteenth birthday celebration tomorrow. In fact, she'd intended to shop for a gift today, and in the excitement of Brian's invitation to Astroworld, she had forgotten that, too.

"I'm afraid I did forget. Well, it can't be helped. I'll call Nicky in the morning and make sure I take his gift over on Tuesday." Tuesday was the actual birthday.

"What could *possibly* be so important that you forgot about Nicky's birthday?"

Leslie counted to ten. "You know, Mother," she finally said, determinedly keeping her voice even and calm, "it's my business what I'm doing, and if I'd wanted to share that information with you, I would have." Before her mother could say anything in retaliation, Leslie continued. "Now I'll let you get back to sleep. Have fun tomorrow, and I'll talk to you in a couple of days."

Her mother said an icy goodbye. Leslie stared at the phone pensively. She knew this was not the end of the subject. The next time she and her mother talked, Peggy would manage to turn the conversation around to Leslie's absence at tomorrow's dinner, because just the fact that Leslie had not said what her other plans were would have alerted her mother to their importance. And once her mother's curiosity was aroused, she would chip away at Leslie until she found out what she wanted to know.

Maybe there would be nothing to tell. Maybe, after tomorrow, she would not see Brian again. Because, after tomorrow, if he made no move to initiate another meeting between them, she could not.

She'd done it once, tonight.

But no more.

If he didn't want to continue the relationship, she would not force herself upon him.

She still wasn't sure why she had issued *this* invitation, especially when she knew darn well she was bound to get hurt by the relationship. Maybe it was because today had been such a good day, and he had seemed to enjoy being with her as much as she'd enjoyed being with him.

Or maybe it's just that hope springs eternal in the human breast, she thought wryly. *All evidence and rational thinking to the contrary...*

Jeffrey didn't know when the idea had come to him, but sometime during the day at Astroworld he'd looked at his dad laughing the way he used to laugh when his mother was alive, and he'd realized his dad was happy, *really* happy.

He liked it when his dad was happy, 'cause then he felt happy, too. For such a long time, his dad was so sad. He would pretend he wasn't, but Jeffrey knew. He could see the sadness in his dad's eyes, and sometimes, when his dad thought Jeffrey wasn't looking, he'd look like he was going to cry. It made Jeffrey's chest hurt when his dad looked like that, and then *he* wanted to cry, too. It was awful.

But today was different. Today his dad didn't look sad at all. And Jeffrey was pretty sure he knew the reason why. It was because Leslie was with them. She was the one making his dad happy.

He remembered what his dad had said about Leslie being like his mother. His dad was right. Leslie was a lot like his mom. Jeffrey thought about that for a while. And suddenly, he realized that maybe his mom really *had* heard him when he prayed to her. He'd thought she hadn't, but maybe, like Reverend McNatt had said in one of his sermons, prayers could get answered in different ways.

Maybe Leslie was the answer to his prayer.

That night, Leslie dreamed of Brian once again. In her dream, she and Brian and Jeffrey were in church together, Brian on one side of her and Jeffrey on the other. They were holding hands and all around them, people were smiling at them. The dream gave her such a good feeling that when she awakened on Sunday morning, she was filled with a tremulous hope.

Maybe things *could* work out between them. Maybe she'd been wrong, and Brian really was ready for a new relationship. How wonderful it would be to have Brian in her life, because he didn't come alone. He also had a child she already loved, a child she would be proud to call her own.

She knew she shouldn't allow herself to fantasize this way. Hadn't she learned a long time ago that real life rarely turns out the way we hope it will?

But one never knew.

She decided today would be the test. The way Brian acted today would tell her, one way or the other, whether there was any future for her in this relationship.

And if there wasn't, then she had better move on.

As Leslie prepared for Brian and Jeffrey's arrival, she decided some good had come from Elliott's demands for perfection. At least now she knew how to cook and entertain.

She was the one who wanted everything to be perfect this evening. She wanted to impress Brian with her abilities and competence, to feel that here, finally, was a man who recognized her talents and her value. She wanted compliments and admiration.

After dusting and vacuuming, she mopped the kitchen floor and cleaned the guest bathroom until it shone. When she was finished, she started her sauce. Getting out her Dutch oven, she poured in a bit of olive oil and turned the burner on medium low heat. Then she quickly chopped onions and added them and a couple of teaspoons of minced garlic to the heated oil. She knew purists chopped fresh garlic, but she'd found the bottled minced garlic worked just as well, and it was a lot easier and faster.

Once the onions and garlic were simmering, she poured in several large cans of tomato sauce, followed by a couple of cans of tomato puree. After mixing thoroughly, she added fresh basil and oregano, sugar, salt, and pepper.

With the sauce slowly cooking, she began making her ground turkey meatballs, which she browned in a skillet, then added to the sauce.

That done, she got out the ingredients to make pie crust dough from scratch—another skill acquired at Elliott's insistence. While the crust baked, she assembled everything she'd need for a lemon filling, because in her experience, no one disliked lemon meringue pie.

By three o'clock, she was finished. A mixed green salad was ready and chilling in the refrigerator. A loaf of French bread had been sliced, buttered, and sprinkled with garlic—ready to pop into the oven just before dinner. The sauce had thickened, the meatballs were thoroughly cooked, and the pie sat cooling on a wire rack.

Next she set the kitchen table, deciding that tonight's dinner would be more comfortable for both Brian and Jeffrey if it was informal. Still, she wanted the table setting to look nice, so she angled a square yellow tablecloth on her round oak kitchen table and in the center placed a blue and white earthenware pitcher filled with yellow roses from her garden. Her dark blue dishes, yellow cloth napkins, and everyday stainless cutlery completed her preparations.

Now all she would have to do was cook the pasta, reheat the sauce, and warm the bread.

Well satisfied with her efforts, she headed upstairs to shower and dress.

Despite all his misgivings and his resolve not to see Leslie again after tonight, Brian had to admit he was looking forward to the dinner at her house. He and Jeffrey hadn't had much of a social life this past year, and it was nice to be going somewhere other than Jeffrey's grandparents' or Brenda's. Once again he realized how much their lives had changed, and how he had to make more of an effort to see people and do things.

At four-thirty, dressed in casual tan slacks and a light blue cotton shirt, he poked his head into Jeffrey's room to see if he was ready.

"I just gotta comb my hair," Jeffrey said, straightening from tying his sneakers. He wore clean jeans and a striped Tommy Hilfiger shirt.

"You look nice."

Jeffrey grinned. "This is the shirt Gran bought me."

"I know."

They walked downstairs together, and Brian

picked up the bottle of merlot he'd left on the kitchen table.

"What's that for?" Jeffrey said.

"It's a hostess gift for Leslie."

"What's a hostess gift?"

"Well, when you're invited to someone's house for dinner, it's nice to take them a gift. Your mom taught me that."

"Oh," Jeffrey said. "Well, should I give Leslie something, too?"

Brian smiled. "That's not necessary, son. This is a gift from both of us."

"Kids don't give people wine, Dad."

Brian's first impulse was to tell Jeffrey this was not an important distinction, but he curbed it, saying instead, "That's true, but Leslie doesn't expect you to bring her anything, Jeffrey. Only adults bring hostess gifts."

Jeffrey frowned. "But I want to."

"Tell you what. If we leave right now, we'll have time to stop at Schermer's and we'll get a box of candy for you to give her. Okay?"

Jeffrey's eyes brightened. "Okay. Lemme go get my money."

"I've got money. You don't need to get yours."

"Dad," Jeffrey said patiently, "if the candy's from me, then I should pay for it."

Joy would have been so proud of Jeffrey, Brian thought as his son raced back upstairs. He was a wonderful kid—the best of both of them.

And in that moment, Brian knew Joy wasn't really lost to him. How could she be, when so many of the qualities he had loved in her were alive in her son?

They arrived at Leslie's house at two minutes past five.

"Right on time," she said, accepting their gifts with a smile and a solemn handshake for Jeffrey, who beamed. Behind her stood a golden retriever, whose tail wagged enthusiastically.

"You have a dog!" Jeffrey said.

"Yes," she said. "This is Amber. I've had her nearly eleven years."

"I love dogs." Jeffrey bent down to pet her, and the dog licked his face. Jeffrey laughed out loud.

"She's *very* friendly," Leslie said.

Leslie looked great, Brian thought, eyeing the way the black silky pants outfit she wore drifted around her slender figure as she walked.

"How about a house tour first?" she said after depositing the wine and candy on a small mahogany table in the foyer.

"Can Amber come, too?" Jeffrey said.

"Try to keep her away!" Leslie said, laughing.

Brian was fascinated by the house. It completely lived up to his expectations. "They don't make houses like this anymore," he said, running his hand over the intricate molding in the parlor, which sat to the right of the entry hall.

"No, they don't."

"I'll bet it costs quite a bit in upkeep."

She nodded. "Yes. Thank goodness there's no mortgage or anything. That makes it easier. But with a house this old, there's always something needing repair or replacement."

To the left of the entry was a large dining room, outfitted in heavy, old-fashioned furniture.

"The furniture belonged to my grandmother," Leslie explained. "In fact, most of the furniture in the house did. After my divorce, I didn't have much of my own."

The rest of the downstairs consisted of a large, bright kitchen, a walk-in pantry, a room off the kitchen that contained a washer and dryer—Leslie explained that it had originally been a maid's room—a half bath, and a TV room that overlooked a side garden.

"This room used to be a study," she said, "but I hated to put a TV in the front parlor."

Jeffrey, followed by Amber, had walked over to inspect something on a table by the TV set. "It's Nintendo, Dad! Look!"

Leslie smiled at Brian's quizzical look. "For when my nephew and nieces come over." She turned to Jeffrey. "Would you like to play while I show your Dad around upstairs?"

"Can Amber stay here with me?"

"Yes."

"Okay!"

So they settled Jeffrey in front of the TV with the Nintendo game—Amber curled up on the floor by his feet—and Brian followed Leslie up the staircase to the second level.

The upstairs was dissected by a center hallway, just as the downstairs had been. Here there were five bedrooms and two full bathrooms. Two of the bedrooms faced the backyard and two were on either side of the house. Facing the front was one large room ringed with windows. Here there were no bedroom furnishings, only a large rectangular worktable and chair, several easels, a drawing board, a big double sink and drain board, several supply cabinets and bookcases, and dozens of canvases and matted watercolors stacked everywhere. Belatedly, he remembered their conversation at the pizza parlor, when Jeffrey had said she painted houses. He had forgotten it until now.

"My only real extravagance," Leslie said, pointing to the sinks. "I had those installed so I could clean up without having to carry everything downstairs or use one of the bathrooms. Luckily for me, this wall backs up to a bathroom, so the plumbing was already in place."

Brian nodded, but his mind was already drawn to the paintings. He walked to the nearest stack. "Do you mind if I look at them?"

She shook her head. "No."

The paintings amazed him. He'd had no idea she was so talented. How could he? he thought wryly. Every time they'd been together, he had monopolized the conversation, talking about himself or Jeffrey—never her.

"I can see why you've sold some of your paintings. You're good," he said as he studied one she'd done of the Ashbel Smith Building, nicknamed "Old Red" by Galvestonians because of its dark pink color.

"Thank you," she said modestly, but he could see she was pleased by his compliment.

He picked up another of the paintings, which had been matted but not framed. This one was a delicate wash of pastels depicting the Samuel May Williams house. Leslie had painted it as it might have appeared in the late 1800s—with a carriage in front and several ladies in long skirts standing on the front lawn.

"That one's my favorite," she said.

He looked at her. "When do you find the time to do everything? With this house to keep up and your job?"

She shrugged. "Since I'm single and don't have children to worry about, it's not a problem."

"That's going to change if you adopt a child, you know."

"I know, but it'll be a good change."

"I'd hate to see you give up painting, though."

She smiled. "I'll always find time to paint."

With that, they went back downstairs.

After dinner—which was a great success, Leslie thought happily—they installed Jeffrey back at the Nintendo game, and Brian helped Leslie clean up the kitchen.

"You know," he said as he handed her plates to scrape and rinse, "I realized something tonight. In the few times we've been together, I've told you all kinds of things about me, but you've never talked about yourself."

"My mother always told me it was better to be a listener than a talker," she said lightly. She had no intention of talking about herself.

"Well, tonight we're going to reverse things," he said. "*I'm* going to listen, and *you're* going to talk. I want to hear all about Leslie."

She opened the dishwasher and began putting in the plates. "My life is pretty boring."

"Don't think you're going to get away with that. C'mon. Start from the beginning."

She straightened, looking him in the eye. "Really, Brian, there's nothing to tell."

"Of course there is."

She sighed. "You're not going to give this up, are you?"

"Nope."

"Okay." She made a face. "You asked for it. The life of Leslie Marlowe in a nutshell. Born thirty-five years ago right here in Galveston. Parents still live here. Father owns an insurance agency. Mother is a social butterfly. One brother, Nick, four years older. Graduated from a local high school, started college at U.T. in Austin, dropped out the summer after my freshman year. Got married. Married five years. Divorced eleven years ago. Inherited this house one year after the divorce." She smiled. "The rest you know. See? Boring.'' She walked to a nearby cup-board and took out several plastic containers.

"You're not getting off so easily," he said. "What were you studying in college?"

"Art."

He laughed. "That was a stupid question, wasn't it? Well, why'd you drop out?"

"Because I'd met Elliott and we were getting married. He didn't want me to go to school because he said if I did, I wouldn't be able to travel with him."

"How'd you meet? At school?"

Although she only intended to tell him bare facts, once she started, Leslie suddenly found herself tell-ing him everything. "No, not at school. Elliott is from Dallas. I met him because my uncle—my mother's brother—gave me a job at his investment firm for the summer, and Elliott is one of the part-ners there. He was a lot older than me. I was only nineteen, he was thirty-two. He swept me off my feet. He was charming, had lots of money, knew all the right things to do and say." She grimaced. "I didn't stand a chance. Especially since my mother was so enthusiastic. You see, Elliott comes from 'the right sort of people' which is very, very important to my mother. Besides, he charmed her, too. He'd say things like how she couldn't possibly be my mother, why, she looked more like my sister than anything else. And, of course, he was rich. That, too, is important to my mother. My dad had misgivings. Privately, he told me he thought Elliott was too old for me and urged me to think about it some more, but unfortunately, I didn't pay attention to him.'' She sighed. ''The marriage was a disaster. The problem was, Elliott didn't really love me. He thought I was young enough and malleable enough that he could mold me into the kind of wife he wanted. But what he wanted was perfection, and I was far from perfect.''

She told him about the lunch at Gaido's and the dinner party with the cockroach. She told him how Elliott belittled her and criticized her and made her feel as if she was stupid and worthless. And she told him about the miscarriages. ''So now you know the whole pitiful story,'' she said when she finally wound down. ''Aren't you glad you asked?''

He shook his head slowly. ''What a bastard.''

''Well, yes, he is, but I can't blame him for everything,'' she said. ''After all, nobody was holding a gun to my head and making me stay with him all those years. I had several years of therapy after the divorce, and that was the best thing I ever did for myself. I learned so much about myself and how unresolved issues with our parents often lead us to choose the same kind of relationship with a spouse. But you know, the experience with Elliott wasn't all bad. I believe I'm stronger for it, so maybe I should thank him.''

''You're a better person than I am if you can feel that way.''

''What's the point in being bitter? Or feeling

sorry for myself? I made a mistake, I paid for it, I learned from it.''

''Do you ever hear from him now?''

''No. Although through my uncle I know Elliott remarried as soon as our divorce was final.'' She smiled sardonically. ''Seems there was a new young receptionist at the firm and he must have had his eye on her for some time, seeing as how she presented him with a bouncing baby boy less than five months later.'' She said this lightly, because she did not want Brian to feel sorry for her, and that particular hurt had long since faded.

Even so, she averted her eyes and began to spoon the leftover sauce and meatballs into the largest of the plastic containers. She was suddenly sorry she'd said so much.

''Leslie,'' he said, walking up behind her. He touched her shoulder. ''I'm glad you told me.''

Slowly, she turned. His expression caused her breath to catch and her heart to begin a slow tattoo. He wanted to kiss her. She could see the desire in his eyes. She swallowed. Heat suffused her, and she swayed toward him.

''Leslie…'' His voice sounded rough.

She wet her lips.

His throat worked, and he took a step backward. ''I think we need to talk.''

For a moment, she was incapable of speech. Then, from somewhere, she summoned the strength to nod and say, ''Want some coffee?''

''Sure.''

She could feel his eyes on her as she filled the coffeemaker. She told herself to get a grip. But she couldn't forget that look in his eyes. And she couldn't banish the ache of disappointment or the need that pulsed through her. It had been so long since she had felt this way. So long. And she wanted Brian so much. What would it be like to be held by him? To feel his lips against hers? To have him touch her?

Behind her, she heard him clear his throat. "Leslie."

She turned. Meeting his eyes was very nearly her undoing, but she managed to overcome her intense desire to fling herself into his arms and instead walked calmly over to the table where he now sat.

"The last couple of days, they've been great," he said softly.

Leslie knew what was coming. She heard the "but." Her disappointment intensified, even though she had known from the start there was no future for her with this man.

"I'm very attracted to you, I think you know that, but I'm not the kind of man who can have a casual sexual relationship, and I know you're not that kind of woman, either."

"No," she whispered, although at that moment, she wasn't sure she wouldn't give him anything he asked for.

"But even if we were," he continued, "there's Jeffrey to consider." He paused, looked beyond her. Then slowly, his eyes met hers again. "If I ever get involved with a woman again, it'll be a total commitment. But I'm just not ready for that now.''

"I know," she said, but she was no longer sure it was true. She thought he was just scared. Scared and running away.

"The thing is, though, you're important to Jeffrey, and your friendship has already become important to me."

"I feel the same way."

"So what do you think?" he said, giving her a sad smile. "Do you think we can just be friends?"

"We're *already* friends, and I don't want to lose that friendship, either," she answered.

He smiled, and she could see the relief in his eyes. Reaching across the table, he took her hand. "You're a wonderful person, Leslie. You're going to make some man a terrific wife." So saying, he released her hand.

Those words were her death knell, Leslie knew. And even though it cost her every ounce of strength and courage she possessed, she managed to smile. "Thanks, Brian. You'll make some woman a terrific husband...someday."

Chapter Nine

"I really like Leslie's house," Jeffrey said on the way home.

"Do you?"

"Uh-huh. Her dog's pretty neat, too."

Brian heard the wistfulness in Jeffrey's voice. He knew how much Jeffrey would like to have a dog, but their house had no real yard to speak of. It sat on a sandy knoll across the street from beachfront homes, and it wasn't fenced. Brian had always thought it wouldn't be practical to have a dog, but maybe they could get a small dog. One that could be indoors most of the time.

"Didn't you like her house, Dad?"

"Yes, I did."

Brian was still fighting feelings of guilt over his

reaction to Leslie tonight. What was wrong with him that he couldn't seem to control his feelings? He knew Leslie was wrong for him. Probably the only reason he was attracted to her was because she reminded him of Joy. But even as he thought this he knew down deep it wasn't entirely true, because the more he was around Leslie, the more he realized how different the two women were.

All right, tonight he'd reacted to Leslie in a visceral way. And that reaction, that desire to kiss her, had nothing to do with reminders of Joy. The simple truth was, he'd wanted Leslie. Even so, he knew he'd done the wisest thing by pulling back. Because he'd told her the truth. He wasn't the kind of man who could have a casual sexual relationship, even if it had been possible, given his situation. And she wasn't that kind of woman.

"Dad?"

Brian gave himself a mental shake. "Hmm?"

"Do you think *we* could get a dog?"

"You know, I was just thinking about that."

"You were?"

"Uh-huh."

"Dad!"

"Now let's not get too excited. I think we should talk to Edie first. Because she'd be the one taking care of a dog most of the time."

"She likes dogs, I know she does."

"Well, liking dogs and taking care of a dog are two different things, Jeffrey. A dog is a big responsibility."

"I'd take care of it, Dad!"

Brian smiled. "I know you think you would, but a good bit of the time, you're in school."

"But when I'm home, I'd do everything. I'd feed him and give him water and play with him."

"We still have to talk to Edie before we make a decision."

"But if she says yes, we could get one?" Jeffrey's voice climbed higher with each word, he was so excited.

"Let's just say we'll look into the possibility."

"Dad! That would be so great! I want a dog just like Leslie's."

"Now wait a minute, Jeffrey. We couldn't get a dog like Leslie's, not where we live. A dog that big needs a yard to run around in. No, we'd need to get a small dog, a house dog."

"That's okay. I don't care. I like small dogs. Where will we go to get him?"

Brian couldn't help smiling. "We'll probably just go to one of the pet shelters and see what they have."

"Maybe Leslie could go with us. She knows lots about dogs."

Brian decided in wry amusement that it wouldn't have mattered if he'd decided he never wanted to see Leslie again, because obviously Jeffrey had other ideas.

By now they'd reached their house, and Brian opened the garage with his automatic door opener and pulled the Suburban in. He hadn't even shut off the engine before Jeffrey had his seat belt unbuckled and had hopped out. Brian heard the phone ringing when Jeffrey opened the door leading into the house.

"I'll get it," Jeffrey said.

"Okay."

A few seconds later, just as Brian entered the house, he heard Jeffrey shout, "Grandpa! Hi! Guess what? We might get a dog!"

Brian smiled at Jeffrey's exuberance. No matter what the reason, it was good to see his son so happy. Brian walked into the kitchen where Jeffrey stood near the counter where they kept the cordless phone unit.

"Yeah, Dad said if Edie likes dogs, then we can get one. Isn't that great?"

Brian knew the dog question was already settled.

"Oh, yeah, well, we were at Leslie's house," Jeffrey said.

Brian froze. Hank must have tried to get them earlier and asked Jeffrey where they had been. Now he or Theresa would be sure to ask Brian about Leslie, and Brian wasn't ready to tell him. *Damn! Why couldn't I have answered the phone?*

"Leslie works for Dr. Singer," Jeffrey said, oblivious to the turmoil now going on inside Brian.

"She's my friend," he continued. "She went to Astroworld with me and Dad yesterday, and she made spaghetti for us today. She's really neat, Grandpa. You'd like her. She lives in this really cool house. It's got something called a widow's walk way up on top—she told us all about it—and all these neat seats in the windows and she has a big dog that I played with and she even has a Nintendo.'' All this was said without a breath.

Brian wanted to kick himself for not paving the way with Hank and Theresa. He should have explained about Leslie the last time they'd talked. He could just imagine what they would think about Jeffrey's enthusiastic report of the evening.

Jeffrey went on and on, extolling Leslie's virtues. Finally, he wound down, said a still-excited goodbye to his grandfather, and handed the phone to Brian. ''I'm goin' upstairs,'' he said, taking off. Brian waited until he heard his sneakers clomping on the stairs before he spoke. ''Hello, Hank.''

''Hello, Brian. I hear you've had a big weekend.''

Was it Brian's imagination, or did his father-in-law's voice seem cooler? Brian girded himself for the questions he knew would follow, telling himself not to feel guilty. He had done nothing wrong. Yet he knew he had every reason to feel guilty. He might not have acted on his desires, but they were still there. If the Paladinos were to suspect his feelings, they would be hurt immeasurably. And he couldn't blame them. Joy had only been dead fourteen months, and already their son-in-law was thinking about another woman. More than thinking. *Wanting* another woman!

Despite all these turbulent thoughts, he managed to speak lightly. ''Yes, we've been busy. What about you? How'd the fishing go this week?''

''Fine, fine,'' Hank said.

"And the weather?"

"The weather's been great. A bit cool at night, but wonderful during the day."

"It's been hot here."

"Yes, we've been watching the weather."

"Well, we miss you," Brian said.

"We miss you, too. So…you guys are doing all right without Edie?"

"More than all right. We're having fun being together."

"So I heard." Hank paused. "Who is this Leslie person Jeffrey kept talking about?"

Trying not to betray by any change in tone or inflection that the question had any significance, Brian said, "She's Dr. Singer's office manager, and Jeffrey has gotten quite attached to her." Brian explained that he'd discussed this attachment with Dr. Singer and what Dr. Singer had said.

"How old a woman is she?"

"She's in her middle thirties."

"I see," he said thoughtfully.

Brian knew Hank suspected there was more to this than Brian was telling him, but Brian had no intention of going into the situation any further until the Paladinos came home at the end of August. Maybe by then the whole thing would be resolved and there'd be no need to explain anything else.

They talked for a few minutes more, then Hank put Theresa on the phone. "I didn't get to talk to Jeffrey," she said.

"He went up to his bedroom, but I'll call him,"

Brian said, relieved he wouldn't have to answer yet more questions.

After Jeffrey talked to his grandmother and then headed back to his room, Brian walked to the kitchen window and stared out. He was frustrated and mad at himself. The Paladinos were wonderful people. They had been completely supportive of him from the very beginning, more like parents than in-laws. They didn't deserve to feel one moment of anxiety because of him or anything he did.

Yet how else could Brian have handled this situation, given Jeffrey's feelings for Leslie?

That night, after Jeffrey was asleep, Brian lay awake in his big, lonely bed. For a long time, he thought about the events of the past week, starting from the moment he'd stepped into Dr. Singer's office and seen Leslie for the first time. He simply didn't see any way he could have done anything different.

And really, if he didn't feel this attraction to Leslie, would he even be this worried about it? The honest answer was no. He would have been able to discuss her and Jeffrey's attachment to her with Hank and Theresa and not felt a single qualm. *It's you who's causing the real problem,* he told himself ruefully.

Brian wondered again if maybe it would be better all around to switch Jeffrey to another therapist and sever all ties with Leslie. But after tossing and turning for hours, he knew he couldn't do it. Much as he valued the Paladinos, and much as he didn't want to cause them any more pain—and despite the fact that this solution would make things easier for *him*—Jeffrey was the most important person in this entire scenario. And losing Leslie's friendship would hurt Jeffrey too much.

Brian was just going to have to tough it out. He was going to have to keep his own desires tamped down and he was going to have to cope with the guilt he felt and he would have to make damn sure that from now on he didn't say or do anything that would complicate the situation any more than it already was.

Jeffrey couldn't sleep. He still couldn't believe his dad had said yes about getting a dog. It was gonna be so cool to have a dog. He could take a dog across to the beach and they could run, and Jeffrey could throw a stick and the dog could fetch it. Maybe Jeffrey could even get a Frisbee and teach his dog to catch it the way he'd seen guys on TV with their dogs.

He couldn't wait to tell Leslie about the dog. 'Cause if it wasn't for her, he wouldn't be getting one. Boy, ever since his dad had met Leslie, things had been different. His dad was happier and now they were getting a dog. It was just like when his mother was alive. If his dad had said no about something, and his mother thought they should do it, she'd just smile at him and talk to him and pretty soon his dad would be smiling too and saying, ''Joy, you sure know how to twist me around your little finger.''

When Jeffrey was little, he'd wonder how his mom could do that. Her little finger was really little, and his dad was big. Then when he got older, one day he asked his dad about it, his dad had said it was just a figure of speech. When Jeffrey had asked him to explain what a figure of speech was, his dad started to laugh and said he really couldn't, that it was just a way of saying something, just like Jeffrey's grandmother always said it was raining cats and dogs. That was a figure of speech, too.

Grown-ups were so funny. Half the time they said one thing and meant another, although Jeffrey's dad was a whole lot better about telling him the truth than some of his friend's dads. Leslie was like that, too. When she talked to Jeffrey, she didn't talk to him like he was a kid. She talked to him like he was a grown-up, just like his mom had.

Boy, wouldn't it be neat if now that his mom was gone, Leslie could be his mom? His dad liked her, so maybe it could happen. If his dad married Leslie, they could probably even live in her house. Jeffrey grinned. By that time, they'd probably have their dog, so then there'd be *two* dogs to play with!

He fell asleep with the smile still on his face.

Leslie couldn't sleep. Until the end, the evening had been so wonderful. Having Brian and Jeffrey in her home, sitting in the kitchen just like they were a family, had felt so right. She had only known

Brian little more than week, yet she felt entirely comfortable with him, as if they'd been friends for years.

And then everything had gone wrong.

Now Leslie wasn't sure what would happen. Brian had said he wanted to be friends, but what did that mean, really? Would they continue to spend time together?

Leslie hoped so.

Because as long as she could continue to see him, there was a chance things might eventually work out.

Edie came back armed with pictures of the new grandson and filled with tales of her week in Ohio. "But I missed you a lot," she told Jeffrey, ruffling his hair affectionately. "Tell me all about your week."

"I'll let him tell you, and I'll be off to work," Brian said, draining his coffee cup. He rose from the table where Jeffrey had just sat down to a breakfast of scrambled eggs and cinnamon rolls.

"But Dad, you said you'd ask Edie about the dog," Jeffrey said.

"I was planning to wait until tonight. Let Edie catch her breath first."

"What dog?" Edie said.

"Dad said we could get a dog," Jeffrey said eagerly. "If you say it's okay."

Edie looked at Brian.

Brian sighed. Then he explained. "It's up to you,

Edie. You'll be the one doing the most work, I'm afraid.'' He could see from her face she was less than enthusiastic about the idea.

She looked at Jeffrey, whose face shone with hope. Brian knew the exact moment when her defenses collapsed. She squeezed Jeffrey's shoulder. ''Getting a dog means a lot to you, doesn't it?'' she said softly.

''I want a dog more than anything,'' Jeffrey said fervently.

''Well, then…'' She smiled. ''I think you should get one.''

The smile on Jeffrey's face was all the reward a person could ask for, Brian thought as he gave Edie a look of thanks. She nodded, and Brian knew they were in perfect agreement. Anything that could put that light back in Jeffrey's eyes was worth doing, no matter what the cost.

Leslie knew it would be unrealistic to hope she would hear from Brian on Monday. So when she didn't, she told herself not to be disappointed. Yet she was. He could have called to say thank-you for the previous evening. There would have been no obligation for him to say anything more.

But you know there would.

If he called, he would have felt he should extend some kind of invitation to her. That's the way things were done. Otherwise, a man simply didn't call.

He didn't call on Tuesday, either.

By Wednesday, Leslie decided he wasn't going

to. She tried to focus her mind on her appointment with the adoption agency that afternoon and away from Brian and Jeffrey. For the most part, she was successful.

And then, at eleven-thirty, he called. Just the sound of his voice caused her to get a weak feeling in her chest. "You're going to the adoption agency today, aren't you?" he said.

"Yes."

"Well, I just called to wish you luck."

"Thank you, Brian."

"Let me know how things turn out."

"I will."

"In fact, if you don't have other plans, why don't Jeffrey and I take you to dinner? You can tell me all about it then."

She wanted to say yes so badly. "Oh, Brian, that's so nice of you. But I always volunteer at the children's shelter on Wednesday nights, and they count on me. It's too late to cancel on them. I'm sorry."

"Don't apologize. I understand. Maybe another time."

"Yes," she echoed. "Another time."

She wanted to cry after he'd hung up. *You idiot! Why didn't you just call the shelter and make some excuse?* But she knew she would never do that. They really *did* count on her. There was a terrible shortage of volunteers and not enough money to hire more paid help.

Well, he'd told her to let him know what happened, so it would be perfectly okay for her to give him a call tomorrow. And maybe then he'd issue another invitation. In the meantime, first things first. Right now she needed to think about her upcoming appointment and go over everything she wanted to say.

Brian was glad he'd called Leslie. He'd debated whether he should, but in the end, he'd followed his instincts. And it had been the right thing to do.

He hoped things turned out all right for her today. He knew how badly she wanted a child. And she would make a wonderful mother. Anyone seeing the way she interacted with Jeffrey would have no doubt about that. Even Jeffrey's friend Michael had warmed up to her almost immediately.

At two o'clock, Brian thought about Leslie again. She would be at the adoption agency now. He knew she was nervous, but he felt sure everything would work out fine. Because the folks at the agency would have to be blind not to see that Leslie was the kind of mother every kid should have. She would get the child she wanted. The only question was how long it would take.

It didn't surprise him to learn she did volunteer work at the children's shelter, either. The more he learned about her, the more he realized what a nice person she was, and the more he liked her.

Maybe it was for the best she'd been busy tonight. This way, he could just call her tomorrow, find out how things went, and leave it at that.

* * *

"Hello." Leslie walked up to the receptionist's desk. "I'm Leslie Marlowe. I have a two o'clock appointment."

The young blonde sitting there looked up. She wore a name tag that read Jill Sandstrom. Reaching for a clipboard at the corner of her desk, she said, "Fill this application form out, and when you're finished, I'll let Mrs. Wong know you're here."

It took Leslie more than twenty minutes to fill out the two-page, double-sided form, but finally she finished and returned it to the blonde.

Five minutes later, she was seated in a small inner office across a metal desk from Elizabeth Wong, a tiny woman with beautiful dark eyes and a soft, precise voice. After perusing the form and asking Leslie to expand on some of her answers, Mrs. Wong laid the form down, folded her hands in front of her, and looked at Leslie.

"Tell me, Miss Marlowe, why do you want a child?"

Leslie had thought about this question so much, there was no hesitation in her answer. "Because I don't think anything else in life can compare to the joy of loving and nurturing a child. I have so much love to give, and there are so many children out there who need love." Her heartbeat accelerated as she waited for Mrs. Wong's reaction.

Mrs. Wong studied Leslie for a long moment. Then, just as Leslie began to think she hadn't said what the counselor wanted to hear, Mrs. Wong smiled. "I think you'll make a very good mother," she said.

Leslie's heart soared, and she returned the smile.

Mrs. Wong tapped the application form with one perfectly manicured nail. "It will take a few weeks to do a background check. After that, we'll want to do a home visit. Then, if everything checks out, you'll be put on our waiting list."

"How long after I go on the list will I have to wait?"

Mrs. Wong shrugged daintily. "It depends. You say you are willing to take one of the older children. How old?"

Leslie thought about Jeffrey and how she'd be happy to have a child like him. But realistically, a child of eleven who was available for adoption was likely to have some severe problems. Could she handle that? As a single woman, she would have enough problems to face. "Well, that would depend on the child, I guess. Certainly I'd prefer a baby or toddler, even a three- or four-year-old, but I guess I'd be willing to take one that was older, say maybe six or seven."

"Good. That gives us a good range. If you're *really* willing to take a six- or seven-year-old, you wouldn't have a long wait at all. Perhaps only months. With the younger children, especially babies and toddlers, the wait can be as long as three or four years."

"That long."

Mrs. Wong nodded. "Yes. The younger ones are

in great demand, and it's understandable why. I'm sure you realize from your work at the shelter that older children are apt to have behavioral problems?"

"Yes, I know."

"But because of your work there and your work with Dr. Singer, I think you'd be much better equipped to handle problems than many of our applicants. In fact, I think you're an excellent candidate for adoption, Miss Marlowe."

"Thank you."

As Leslie drove back to the office, her heart felt lighter than it had in years.

Before Leslie had a chance to call Brian Thursday morning, he called the office. Her cheeks warmed with pleasure at the sound of his voice.

"I'm out with the crew today," he said, "and this is the first break I've had."

Leslie could hear the background noise.

"How'd the appointment go yesterday?"

Just as she started to tell him, the other line rang, and she had to put him on hold. When she went back to him, he said, "Listen, it's too hard to talk now. How about tonight? Want to have dinner with us?"

"Oh, that sounds great. What time?" Happiness made her feel positively giddy.

"Six-thirty?"

"That's perfect."

"How does seafood sound? How about Fish-tails?"

"Wonderful."

"Okay, we'll see you then."

For the rest of the day, Leslie practically floated around the office.

"You certainly seem happy today," Dr. Singer commented when the last patient had left.

Leslie smiled. "I am."

"Is there some special reason?"

So Leslie told him about the adoption agency.

"Why, Leslie, I had no idea you were considering something like this."

"I didn't want to say anything until I knew if they would consider me. They'll probably be calling you. Do you mind?"

"Of course I don't mind."

"Do...do you think I'm crazy?"

Dr. Singer shook his head. "No. Why would you think so?"

"Because I'm sure my parents will. Well, my mother will. I don't know about my dad."

"You have to do what you know is right for you, regardless of what they think."

"I know. And this *is* right for me."

He smiled. "You'll make a great mother."

Later, as Leslie prepared to leave, she felt a little guilty, because of course, she hadn't told Dr. Singer the whole truth. Yes, she was happy about the possibility of getting a child. But what had made her so happy today was Brian's invitation, and that was something she wasn't willing to share with Dr. Singer. In fact, today she wasn't willing to share her feelings with anyone. The thing was, she had no idea what was going to happen with her and Brian. Maybe, as they'd discussed on Sunday, the only relationship they would ever have would be as friends.

And if that were the case, Leslie didn't want anyone—not Dr. Singer, not her parents, not even Sandi—feeling sorry for her. Leslie had gone through enough of pitying looks and "poor Leslies" after her divorce to last her a lifetime.

So she was taking no chances.

Time enough to talk about Brian when there was something concrete to tell.

Chapter Ten

For dinner, Brian had chosen a trendy seaside restaurant. Fishtails was located on Seawall Boulevard across from the Flagship Hotel.

"They have great soft-shell crabs here," he said with an apologetic smile. "But it's noisy."

"I told you before, I don't mind noise," Leslie said. "And you're right about the soft-shell crabs. They're wonderful."

Once they were settled at their table, Jeffrey said, "Guess what, Leslie? We're getting a dog."

"You *are?*" She looked at Brian.

He smiled a bit ruefully. "After we left your house Sunday night, Jeffrey twisted my arm."

"I didn't really twist his arm," Jeffrey said seriously. "That's a figure of speech."

Leslie raised her eyebrows. "*I'm* impressed. How do you know about figures of speech?"

"My dad explained about 'em." Then, obviously eager to get back to the important topic, he said, "We're gonna go pick out our dog this weekend."

"Where are you going?"

"I thought we'd try Pet Haven," Brian said, naming a nonprofit shelter in the area. "We're not looking for a purebred or anything. Just a nice, friendly dog."

"I can't wait to get him," Jeffrey said. "He's gonna be my best friend."

"Him?" Leslie teased. "Why not her?"

"I don't want a *girl* dog." His expression was horrified.

"Oh." Leslie fought back a grin. "I see."

"Do you wanna come with us and help us pick out our dog?"

"You're not obligated," Brian interjected quickly, "but you're welcome."

"When were you planning to go?" Leslie tried to gauge whether or not Brian really wanted her along.

"Saturday morning."

"Well…" She turned to Jeffrey, her decision made. "Much as I'd like to be there for this momentous occasion, I'm afraid I can't. I've got an appointment to get a haircut Saturday morning." It was just as well, she thought, glad she had a legitimate excuse, because from now on, unless an invitation was initiated by Brian, she intended to refuse. She didn't want to wear out her welcome.

Just then, their waiter approached, and for the next few minutes, they were busy placing their orders, so Leslie wasn't paying much attention to anything else, and it was only when their waiter left that she realized the empty table next to them had been filled. Shock rippled through her when she saw that her brother and his wife were its occupants.

"Nick!" she said.

Her brother looked around. "Les!" He grinned and touched his wife's shoulder. "Michelle, look who's here." Getting up, he walked over to hug Leslie, who rose, too. Pretty soon, everyone was standing. Leslie introduced Nick and Michelle to Brian and Jeffrey.

"Nice to meet you," Nick said. As the two men shook hands, Nick's blue eyes, so much like their mother's, sized Brian up.

"It's nice to meet you, too," Brian said.

Michelle, who was also blond and blue-eyed, gave Brian one of her warm smiles, but her eyes were filled with curiosity as they turned to Leslie. The two women hugged and Michelle whispered, "Keeping secrets, huh?"

Leslie's mind spun. She did not want her mother to know about Brian. Not yet. Maybe not ever. But unless she wanted to explain why, she couldn't ask Nick and Michelle not to say anything. She also didn't want Nick and Michelle to know about her plan to adopt a child—not until she'd had a chance to talk with her parents—and she didn't plan to do that until she had something definite to report.

"Why don't we ask the waiter to put our two tables together?" Nick suggested.

"Nick," Michelle said, giving him a look. "Maybe they'd rather be alone."

"Oh, no," Leslie said, cheeks coloring.

"No, of course not," Brian said.

As Nick signalled to their waiter, Leslie looked for an opportunity to say something to Brian and managed to whisper in an aside, "Please don't say anything about my appointment at the adoption agency. They don't know yet."

He nodded his understanding, and some of her tension evaporated, but not all. She still had to get through the rest of the evening without giving away her feelings about Brian. That might be tough. Michelle was pretty perceptive, plus she knew Leslie fairly well. Oh, how Leslie wished they had gone somewhere else tonight. She took a deep breath to steady her nerves.

Soon they were all settled at one table. Brian and Nick seemed to hit it off like a house afire, and Michelle, who had a kind heart, was especially sweet to Jeffrey, who warmed to her quickly. Before long he was telling her all about the dog he was going to get.

"I wanted Leslie to go with us, but she's gotta go get her hair fixed," he confided.

Michelle said, "Oh, really?" She raised her eyebrows at Leslie.

"He thinks I'm an expert on dogs because of Amber," Leslie rushed to explain. She immediately realized her mistake. Now Michelle knew that Jeffrey had been in her home. *Stupid, stupid,* she chastised herself, but she simply wasn't used to hiding things. She was by nature an open, honest person.

"Well, Amber is a great dog," Michelle said.

"So how do you two know each other?" Nick said.

"Jeffrey is a patient of Dr. Singer's," Brian said.

"Ah," said Nick.

"Oh," said Michelle.

Leslie knew her sister-in-law was dying to ask all kinds of questions, but thank goodness, she was too polite to do so. Of course, she would have no such qualms once she got Leslie alone.

"Hey, Les, we missed you at dinner on Sunday," Nick said. "Mom didn't have anyone to pick on except me."

Leslie said something innocuous, then quickly, before he or Michelle could ask where she'd been, steered the conversation in another direction. She hoped Brian hadn't put two and two together, figuring out that she'd cancelled a previous commitment at her parents' to have him and Jeffrey over for supper.

"Where are the kids?" she asked.

"Well, Courtney is at camp this week," Michelle said, "and Nicky had a party tonight with a sleepover, and Emma is at Grandma Boudreaux's this week." Michelle's mother lived outside New Orleans.

"One of these weekends I'd like to have Courtney and Emma stay with me." Courtney was nine and Emma was five, and Leslie adored them both.

"Just name the time," Michelle said, laughing. "Want to take them both for the rest of the summer?"

Leslie knew her sister-in-law was teasing. She was a great mother and loved her children.

Although the conversation continued to deal in generalities, Leslie was on tenterhooks throughout the evening. Somehow, though, she made it through without betraying how nervous she was. She wondered what Brian was thinking, but he seemed perfectly relaxed. He and Nick discussed their respective work, the Astros, the proposed renovations to the causeway bridge, Tiger Woods, and the newly appointed head coach of one of the high schools. Of course, Brian didn't have the same things at stake that Leslie did. He wasn't trying to hide their relationship or anything else. *You're the sneaky one here,* she reminded herself.

While they were waiting for their coffee, Michelle said, "Leslie, come with me to the ladies'." Although Leslie would have liked to refuse and thereby postpone the inevitable, she figured she might as well get Michelle's questions over with. Michelle didn't waste time. The minute the two of them were out of earshot, she said, "Where have you been keeping *him* hidden?"

"Shell, it's not what you think," Leslie said.

"Oh? Are you telling me you're *not* interested in Brian? Are you nuts? He's a dream!"

Leslie couldn't help smiling. She realized how silly it would be to try to deny her interest in Brian. Even if she did, Michelle wouldn't believe her. After all, what woman *wouldn't* be interested in him? As Michelle had said, you would have to be nuts.

"Okay," she said as they entered the ladies'. "I admit it. I *am* interested in him, but there are some problems."

"Like what? Is he hiding a wife in the closet or something?"

"No. His wife died about a year ago. That's why Jeffrey has been coming to see Dr. Singer. He was with her when she was killed." Leslie quickly explained about the accident in London.

"Oh, dear," Michelle said, her eyes softening in sympathy. "How awful for them."

"Yes. But there's more." Next Leslie told her about how she reminded Brian of Joy and the problems that had caused. "Even if that complication didn't exist, the bottom line is, he isn't ready for another relationship. He's made that very clear."

Michelle bit her bottom lip. Then she hugged Leslie, holding her close for a long moment. "Don't give up on him," she said. "He really is a great guy, and if he needs time, just hang in there. 'Cause he's worth it."

After they drew apart, Leslie said, "Don't tell Mom and Dad about seeing us tonight, okay? I can't handle Mom's questions. Besides, I'm not sure she'd approve."

Michelle frowned. "Why ever not?"

Leslie sighed. "You know how hung up she is about having the right background."

"So?"

"So Brian's father disappeared before he was born, and his mother abandoned him. He grew up poor in West Texas."

"Oh, for Pete's sake. Is she *really* that shallow that something like that makes a difference?"

"You know she is. Being the right sort is very important to her. She's never forgiven me for 'driving Elliott away' as she put it, because he had the perfect pedigree."

Michelle shook her head in disgust. "Honestly, Leslie, I don't know how you and Nick have put up with her for so long. If my mother acted that way, I'd set her straight in no time."

Leslie could have pointed out that there was nothing for Nick *to* put up with, because her mother had never given him a hard time about anything, but she didn't. After all, it wasn't Michelle's fault that Peggy preferred her son over her daughter, nor that said daughter never measured up to her expectations.

"So what are you going to do if you and Brian *do* get serious?" Michelle asked.

Leslie shrugged. "I guess I'll cross that bridge when I come to it."

"I like your brother and his wife," Brian said.

They had just left the restaurant and were on their

way to Leslie's house. Leslie smiled. "Thanks. I like them, too."

"You haven't told them what you're planning, though?"

"No. I, um, don't want my parents to know right now. They...well, I'm not sure they'll approve." Mindful of Jeffrey in the back seat, Leslie lowered her voice, although he had his earphones on and was listening to his Walkman, so she didn't think he would overhear her, anyway. "Aside from my best friend Sandi, you and Dr. Singer are the only people who do know."

"I'm flattered to be included."

Leslie smiled sheepishly. "You caught me in a weak moment."

"So what *did* happen yesterday?"

"Things went well. They said I was a good candidate. They'll want to visit and do a background check, then I'll get put on the waiting list."

"Leslie, that's great. What kind of wait are they talking about?"

Leslie explained what Mrs. Wong had said.

"You excited?"

"Yes. I am."

"I'm glad things are working out."

"Me, too."

By now they'd reached her street. A few moments later, Brian pulled into her driveway.

"You don't have to walk me to the door," she said, unfastening her seat belt and retrieving her purse from the floor. "Thanks for dinner. I really enjoyed it." She reached for the door handle. "Good night, Jeffrey."

He took off the earphones. "Night, Leslie."

"Of course I'll walk you to the door," Brian said, turning off the ignition. "Wait here, Jeffrey. I'll be right back."

"Okay."

Brian helped her down from the truck, and Leslie loved the feeling it gave her—the feeling of being taken care of. It was a simple thing, and sure, she was an independent woman who had taken care of herself for eleven years, but there was something to be said for having a man in your life. Especially a man like Brian.

"Good luck with finding a dog," she said as they reached the front door.

"I'll call you Saturday," he said, smiling down at her. "Give you a report. That is, if you're going to be home."

"I'll be here." She kept her voice light so she wouldn't betray how happy his words had made her.

"Good night, then." He bent down and kissed her cheek.

After the door closed behind her, she leaned against it and closed her eyes. She could still feel the brush of Brian's lips against her cheek. She knew the kiss hadn't meant anything. It was just a casual way to say good-night to a friend. But her heart didn't care. Her heart was so filled with happiness and thankfulness, she was afraid it might burst.

It wasn't Brian who called on Saturday. It was Jeffrey.

"We got our dog, Leslie!" he shouted. "I want you to come and see him. He's the cutest little puppy."

"I'd love to see him," she said. "Does he have a name yet?"

"Uh-huh. We're gonna call him Charlie."

Leslie smiled. "Charlie's a good name."

Jeffrey went on eagerly, telling her in play-by-play detail just how they'd gone about picking out their dog and everything that had happened since they'd brought him home.

"The first thing he did was pee on the floor," Jeffrey said, giggling.

Leslie laughed, too. "That's the first thing most puppies do when they are taken to a new place."

"I know. Dad told me it's called marking their territory."

"Your dad's pretty smart."

"Yeah. He wants to talk to you, Leslie."

"Hey," Brian said.

Just the sound of his voice made her heart beat faster. "So you got the dog."

"Yeah." He chuckled. "He's a cute little thing. Part beagle and part cocker spaniel."

"Jeffrey's certainly smitten."

"Yes, it was love at first sight." He was silent for a moment. "So, did you get your hair cut?"

She touched the back of her hair. "Yes, I did."

"Not too short, I hope?"

"No. Just a trim."

"Good. I like your hair the way it is."

Leslie knew it was foolish to feel so absurdly pleased by his compliment. "Thanks."

"Do you have plans for the rest of the day?"

Sandi had invited her to spend the evening if she didn't have anything else to do, but Leslie knew she wouldn't mind if Leslie didn't come. In fact, she'd probably cheer if Brian was the reason. "Nothing important."

"We thought we'd take Charlie to the park for a while. Want to come along? Jeffrey can't wait for you to see his dog."

"You sure you want to go to the park? It's awfully crowded on Saturdays in the summer."

"I know, but we don't have a fenced yard, and we'd like to let the dog run around for a while. Wear him out so he'll sleep tonight."

"Instead of the park, why don't you bring him over here? I've got a big backyard. And Amber loves puppies. In fact, why don't you plan to stay for supper tonight? I've got some chicken breasts. We can throw them on the grill."

"That sounds good, but only if you let me bring the rest of the food."

"Why? You bought me dinner on Thursday. It's my turn."

"I insist. I'll just stop at the fried chicken place and pick up mashed potatoes and coleslaw and maybe some beans and biscuits."

"You talked me into it."

"Good. We'll see you in about an hour?"

As good as his word, an hour later, Brian and Jeffrey, accompanied by an adorable, wet-nosed puppy, arrived laden with takeout.

It was a wonderful day.

A golden day.

A perfect day when it seemed to Leslie that nothing bad could ever happen again. The backyard was filled with the sound of Jeffrey's happy laughter and the puppy's yipping and the rumble of Amber's occasional complaint when the puppy got too rambunctious. There was a breeze coming in off the Gulf, and it set her wind chimes to tinkling, and the scent of the climbing roses on the trellis at the side of the garden perfumed the air.

She had unearthed a bottle of chardonnay from the refrigerator, and she and Brian slowly drank the wine and sat in the shade of the back porch while they watched Jeffrey and the two dogs cavort. They talked softly and companionably. At one point, he said, "Your hair looks nice."

Warmth suffused her. "Thanks." She wanted to look at him, but she was afraid her eyes would give away everything she was feeling.

Just then, Jeffrey came running up, his face all flushed and sweaty, saying, "Is there any more lemonade?"

Leslie was grateful for the distraction, and the awkward moment passed.

Around six, Leslie turned on the gas grill and brought out the marinated chicken breasts. Brian said he'd cook and she could get the other stuff ready.

"What other stuff?" she said, laughing. "All I have to do is heat it in the microwave."

He grinned. "So heat already."

She threw an oven mitt at him and ducked when he threw it back.

After they ate and cleaned up, they sat on the porch steps and watched the sun slowly slip over the horizon, and Leslie knew she would never forget this day.

But finally, it came to an end. The puppy fell asleep snuggled next to Amber, both dogs exhausted, and Jeffrey's eyes were drooping, too.

"Guess I'd better get these two home," Brian said.

She helped them gather up everything and walked them out to the Suburban. Jeffrey, holding the sleeping puppy, got into the car.

Brian put his arm around her shoulders and squeezed. "Thanks for having us."

Just that casual touch increased her pulse rate. "It was my pleasure." She wondered if he would kiss her cheek again, but he gave her shoulder another little squeeze, and climbed into the truck.

After that night, a pattern was set. For the rest of June and throughout July, Leslie spent a couple of nights a week with Brian and Jeffrey. She almost always went for pizza with them on Friday nights, and more often than not, she would spend most of Saturday with them. Usually they brought Charlie to her house on Saturdays, just as they had the first time, and then they'd either cook there or Brian would go and get takeout for them.

"Having a puppy is just like having a baby. You can't leave them alone," Brian grumbled, but Leslie knew he loved the dog almost as much as Jeffrey did.

Sometimes Leslie wondered if she wasn't just setting herself up for a terrible fall. But for the most part she was happy, even though it was difficult maintaining the fiction that all she felt for Brian was friendship. He didn't seem to be having any trouble with their agreement, though. In fact, in all the times they'd been together since that night, he had never indicated in any way that he had anything other than friendly feelings for her. Sometimes Leslie thought that Sunday night when she'd thought he wanted to kiss her was a figment of her imagination.

In her saner moments she knew it wasn't. That Sunday night had happened. He had *said* he was attracted to her. She hadn't imagined that.

But maybe he'd changed his mind. Maybe he no longer felt the same way. Why else could he be so relaxed around her? Why else had he never betrayed, even by a flicker in his eyes, that she meant something more to him than a friend?

She wasn't sure she could keep this up indefinitely. Because she had realized something. She wasn't sure exactly when it had happened, but sometime in the past weeks she had gone from thinking she could fall in love with Brian to *being* in love with Brian. And the more she was with him, the deeper and stronger that love became.

And she loved Jeffrey, too. Very much. One of these days, she was going to give away her feelings, and then what?

Brian would bolt. That's what. Then she would be devastated. But what could she do? It was too late to change anything. The damage was already done. Now the only question that remained was when and where the ax would fall that would shatter her emotionally.

During this period, she made sure she never missed Sunday dinner at her parents', at least not because of Brian and Jeffrey. That way she avoided any questions, although one Sunday in mid-July, Michelle managed to get her alone for a few minutes and said, "You still seeing Brian?"

Leslie nodded.

Michelle squeezed her arm. "Good. I've been thinking about you. Sending good thoughts your way."

"Say some prayers, too, will you?" Leslie said, half joking, half serious.

The last week of July Dr. Singer told Leslie he was thinking of terminating Jeffrey. "I'll discuss it with his father, and if he agrees, Friday will be Jeffrey's last session.''

Brian was ecstatic and readily agreed. Leslie was happy for Jeffrey and Brian, too, but she couldn't help wondering if the end of his therapy would mean she would spend less and less time with them. But the day after Dr. Singer talked to Brian, he called and invited her to go to the movies with them, so she decided that particular fear was groundless.

The following week—the first week of August— he called and said they weren't going for pizza on Friday. Instead he invited her to come to dinner at his house.

"Nothing fancy. Just hamburgers on the grill. I'll even do chicken for you if you prefer.''

"No, I like hamburgers.''

"I wasn't going to tell you because I didn't want you to feel obligated to get him anything, but it's Jeffrey's birthday.''

"I never would have forgiven you if you *hadn't* told me,'' she said. She was touched that he wanted her to share Jeffrey's birthday celebration and thrilled that he'd finally invited her to his home. "What time shall I be there?''

"How about six?''

"Perfect. That'll give me time to go home and change.''

The house was easy to find. In fact, so easy, Leslie was there ten minutes early. She had butterflies in her stomach as she walked up the path leading from the driveway at the back of the house to the front.

The house was impressive—a two-story contemporary of weathered gray shingles built on a small rise, so that even though it was several rows back from the beachfront homes, she figured it probably had a great view of the water, especially from the second-floor deck.

Leslie climbed the three steps leading to the first floor deck and rang the doorbell.

A few seconds later, a grinning Jeffrey swung the door wide. "Hi!"

"Hi. Happy birthday."

"Thanks."

She handed him the gift she'd bought: a small, computerized handheld game.

"Dad says I have to wait till we have the cake before I can open my presents."

By now, Brian had walked up behind Jeffrey. Their eyes met, and Leslie's heart fluttered the way it always did when she saw him. "Hi," she said with a catch in her breath.

He smiled. "Hi. C'mon in."

The house was open and bright, with dozens of long-paned windows. As Brian led her through the rooms, giving her the "nickel tour," she saw it was also functional, which any house on the beach needed to be.

The first floor consisted of an L-shaped living room–dining room combination that extended the full width of the house on one side, a guest bath, a utility room, and a large eat-in kitchen that was bright and attractive.

They ended in the living room, where the first thing Leslie noticed was a beautiful portrait of Brian, Joy, and Jeffrey that graced the mantel. She stopped in front of it, unable to wrest her eyes away.

The perfect family, Leslie thought. In the portrait, Joy was sitting on a velvet chair, Jeffrey at her side, with Brian standing behind her. His right hand was on her shoulder. All three were smiling. Joy, dressed in a V-necked black dress, looked radiant, her hazel eyes shining, her smile luminous.

No wonder he loved her, Leslie thought with a sinking heart. Joy was beautiful and aptly named, the kind of woman who would effortlessly attract people to her.

She couldn't imagine why Brian had said she was like Joy. Leslie wasn't at all like Joy. Joy was a woman who was sure of her place in the world. Leslie, on the other hand, was still trying to find hers.

He'll never love me, she thought, stricken. *How could he, after her?*

"What a beautiful portrait," she finally said, amazed she could sound so normal when inside she was dying. Because she suddenly couldn't look at the portrait anymore, she walked over to the grand piano, which sat in one corner in front of the windows and idly touched the keys.

"The piano was Joy's," Brian said from behind her.

Naturally.

"Yeah," Jeffrey piped up, "my mom could really play."

Leslie nodded just as if, with each word, they weren't pounding nails into her coffin. Desperately searching for some other topic, she admired the framed photograph of an older couple that sat on top of the piano.

"Are these your grandparents?" she said, turning to Jeffrey.

"Uh-huh. Grandma and Grandpa Paladino."

Leslie studied their faces. She could see traces of Joy in both. The mother had the same sweet face and the same petite figure. The father had the same eyes. "When do they get back home?"

"The end of the month," Brian said. "Now, do you want to see the rest of the house?"

"I'd love to." Anything to get out of here and away from all these reminders of Joy.

But as Brian proudly showed her the bedrooms—the master and Jeffrey's, plus one guest room—she knew every room contained reminders of Joy. It was obvious a woman had decorated the rooms. She wouldn't have been at all surprised to open the closet in the master bedroom and find Joy's clothes still there.

You are such a fool. Why are you doing this to yourself? He is never going to forget her.

Despair filled her heart.

She shouldn't have come.

She wondered if she could make some kind of

excuse. Maybe say she felt sick. Then she could go home where she belonged.

She'd been kidding herself all summer.

She didn't belong here.

And now she knew she never would.

Chapter Eleven

"Leslie? Is something wrong?" Brian's voice was filled with concern.

Oh, God. Pull yourself together! "No, nothing's wrong." But she avoided his eyes, because she knew she was a terrible liar.

"You sure?"

She nodded. "I—I just have a headache, that's all." As much as she wanted to bolt, she knew she couldn't go home. Jeffrey would be crushed. She couldn't hurt his feelings that way. She would have to tough it out. After all, she'd known the rules of the game from the very beginning. Brian had been up-front with her. He'd told her he wasn't ready for a romantic relationship, and he'd asked her if she thought they could just be friends. *You said yes. Now you have to live with that.*

But Leslie knew she couldn't go on this way. If she did, it would eventually destroy her.

She was lying.

There was something wrong.

For the rest of the evening, he watched her, and it was obvious to him that she wasn't herself. She tried hard, he'd give her that. And there were moments, like when Jeffrey opened her gift—a new computerized game—and exuberantly hugged her, that she looked genuinely happy, but the moments didn't last.

So when she said her headache had returned and if Brian and Jeffrey didn't mind, she'd go home a little early, Brian didn't try to talk her into staying longer. He was disappointed, because he'd thought after Jeffrey had gone to bed for the night, the two of them could sit out on the second-floor deck. He'd imagined them drinking wine in the moonlight, talking quietly and listening to the sound of the waves. He'd been looking forward to it.

The sun was sinking low in the west as he walked her outside. "It's going to be a spectacular sunset," he said. Then lightly, "Sure you don't want to stay and watch it with me?"

Her throat worked and she averted her eyes. She opened her car door.

"Leslie." He touched her shoulder. "I know something's bothering you. I wish you'd tell me what it is. Is it something I said? Something I did?"

She finally looked at him. "Don't be silly, Brian. I just don't feel well, that's all."

He knew that wasn't all, but what could he do? If she didn't want to talk to him, he couldn't force her. He bent forward, intending to kiss her cheek, but she jerked back as if he'd tried to burn her and hurriedly got into her car.

Totally bewildered now, he said, "I'll call you tomorrow." They had talked about going to the Museum of Natural History in Houston. There was a new IMAX film there about vintage airplanes that Jeffrey was eager to see.

She nodded and started the car. "All right. Good night."

"Good night." He stood there until her car disappeared from view, then walked slowly back into the house.

Leslie cried herself to sleep. The following morning, she felt like someone had pounded on her head all night. Looking at her swollen eyes in the bathroom mirror, she was disgusted with herself.

"You knew from the beginning that you were taking an awful chance, letting yourself fall for him," she muttered. "Serves you right."

If only she could make a clean break. Just stop seeing Brian completely. It would be hard, and it would hurt like crazy, but eventually, she would get over it.

But how could she?

There was Jeffrey to consider, and he would not

understand it if she just disappeared from his life. She couldn't hurt him that way. He had already been hurt too much.

She closed her eyes, leaning her forehead against the cool mirror.

She was stuck.

The only thing she could do to protect herself, without causing Jeffrey too much pain, was to gradually pull away from them. Instead of accepting every invitation Brian issued, she could start saying no occasionally, and then more often, until finally the break was complete. She could also move her trip to New York up from October to September. Sandi wouldn't mind, especially if she knew the reason.

Leslie sighed and opened her eyes. Wearily, she washed her face and brushed her teeth.

That's what she would do, then. Gradually pull away.

Starting today.

Brian listened to the phone ringing. After the tenth ring, he slowly replaced the receiver. It was almost noon, and he'd tried calling Leslie at least three times this morning. There had been no answer. Her answering machine wasn't turned on, either.

He hoped she was all right. He'd worried about her all night. He wondered if he and Jeffrey should just drive over there, maybe check things out. Maybe she was too ill to answer the phone.

No, he was being ridiculous. She was probably

just out. But he couldn't help feeling hurt that she'd gone somewhere when they'd practically made plans to go to Houston today.

"Isn't Leslie answering, Dad?"

Brian turned to see Jeffrey standing in the doorway leading from the kitchen to the center hallway. He hadn't heard him come downstairs. "No, she's not. I guess she had to go somewhere."

"Are we still gonna go to Houston?"

"Do you want to?"

Jeffrey thought about it for a few seconds, then shook his head. "Nuh-uh. I'd rather wait till Leslie can go, too."

So would Brian. "Okay. Maybe we'll try for next Saturday."

"What about tomorrow? Why can't we go then?"

"Leslie's pretty busy on Sundays. You know, she goes to church and then she likes to go have dinner with her family."

She didn't really, but she was a dutiful daughter. He admired that about her. He knew, because she'd told him little things over the past six weeks, that her mother gave her a rough time. In fact, her mother sounded pretty hard to take. But Leslie kept hanging in there. He'd asked her about it once, and she'd given him a wry smile and said, "I'm not going to let her walk all over me, but she is my mother, and I love her, faults and all."

That's the way it should be with families, he thought. You didn't have to always agree, but you should still love each other and try to overlook each other's faults.

"Okay, Dad," Jeffrey said. "We'll wait till next Saturday."

Leslie stayed out all day. She went to the office supply store and bought supplies for Dr. Singer's office, she went to the bookstore and stocked up on paperbacks, she went to the pet store and bought dog food and dog biscuits, she went to Wal-Mart, and she killed a couple of hours at the mall. Finally, hot and tired, with sore feet, she headed for home.

The phone was ringing as she walked in the door. She put her packages down and debated answering it. But it might be Brian, and she didn't want to talk to him. Not today.

But what if it wasn't Brian? What if it was Sandi? Or another of her friends? She walked to the phone and put her hand on the receiver, but she still didn't pick it up.

She should have turned on her answering machine. But she hadn't wanted to call Brian back if he called. Sighing, she ignored the ringing and finally it stopped. Only then did she switch on her machine.

After that, she put away the things she'd bought, then headed upstairs. She intended to take a nice, cool shower, put on something comfortable, and spend the evening reading one of her new books.

And if the phone rang, she would let the machine pick up.

* * *

She was avoiding him.

In frustration, Brian banged down the receiver. What had he *done?*

Leslie lingered at her parents' house far past the time she normally stayed on Sundays. And when she finally did leave, she didn't go home. Instead, she headed for Sandi's.

"Leslie!" Sandi said, a welcoming smile on her face. "Come on in." She was barefoot and wore faded cutoffs and a royal blue T-shirt. "What perfect timing. Greg just mixed up some margaritas."

"Be still my heart," said Leslie.

Greg and Sandi lived in a sprawling multilevel house in Pirate's Cove, overlooking the golf course. It was very open and bright, filled with comfortable contemporary furniture and done in shades of cream and ochre and pale green. It had a calm, peaceful ambiance—something Leslie needed after an afternoon spent with her mother.

Five minutes later, shoes off and feet tucked under her, she relaxed against the deep cushions of the living room sofa and sipped her margarita. "Ahh," she sighed. "Heaven." She looked at Greg, who was sitting Indian fashion on the floor, playing with one of his and Sandi's three cats. "Greg, have I told you lately that I love you?"

He grinned. "But will you respect me in the morning?"

Leslie laughed and threw him a kiss.

"Quit flirting with my husband," Sandi said lazily from the depths of her favorite leather chair.

Leslie gave her a mock frown. "You're no fun."

They continued to talk casually for about thirty minutes, then Greg excused himself. "Gotta go check my e-mail. Besides, I know you gals want to talk." He dropped a kiss on Sandi's head as he walked by. "Just yell when you're hungry and I'll go pick up some food for us."

"Thanks, sweetie," Sandi said, giving him a fond smile.

Once he was out of earshot, Sandi turned her astute green gaze to Leslie. "Okay, girlfriend, what's up?"

So Leslie told her everything, up to and including what had happened Friday night. Sandi listened quietly, saying nothing until Leslie was finished. "Is that all?"

"Isn't that enough?" Leslie countered.

Sandi finished off her margarita, then leaned forward. "Tell me, dear heart, what exactly has changed since you first started spending time with Brian and Jeffrey?"

"I'm not sure I understand what you mean."

"Yes, you do."

Leslie chewed on her lower lip. "All right. I guess I finally faced the truth. That's what's changed."

"I don't think so."

"Sandi! Why are you giving me a hard time?"

Sandi sighed. "Because I care about you. Because I want you to *really* face the truth."

"Wh-what do you mean?"

"I mean that yesterday you got scared. You looked at the picture of Joy and saw Joy's house and all Joy's things and suddenly you were afraid you would never measure up. Shoot, it doesn't surprise me. After the job your mother's done on you all these years and the job Elliott did on you, I figured you'd have relapses now and then."

Leslie stared at Sandi. She wanted to say Sandi didn't know what she was talking about. But somehow she couldn't, because what Sandi had said felt too much like the truth.

"Trust me," Sandi said softly. "And the next time Brian calls, you forget all this nonsense. Because despite that garbage he told you about just wanting to be friends, down deep, that isn't what he really wants. And one of these days, he's going to realize it. Don't you want to be there when he does?"

About seven-thirty, Greg went out and picked up chicken enchiladas from a neighboring Tex-Mex place. They ate and listened to music, and Leslie didn't get home until after ten. She hadn't been in the house five minutes when the phone rang. She knew before she answered that it would be Brian.

"I've been calling you all weekend," he said, a note of accusation in his voice. "I was afraid something had happened to you."

"I'm sorry you were worried. I—I had a lot of things to do, so I was out most of the time."

"Did you forget we'd talked about going to the Museum of Natural History yesterday?"

"I'm afraid I did." Well, of course. She'd been so busy feeling sorry for herself, how could she have remembered? "I hope you and Jeffrey went anyway."

"He didn't want to go without you."

Now she felt like a heel. "I'm sorry," she said again, knowing it was inadequate.

He was silent for a long moment. Then, in a softer voice, he said, "You okay?"

"Yes, I'm fine."

"You sure?"

"Positive."

"I thought you were mad at me."

She sighed. "No, Brian, I wasn't mad at you." She knew he wanted her to explain, but how could she? *The thing is, I'm crazy about you, Brian, and Friday, when I saw the life you'd had with Joy, how beautiful she was, how happy you all were, I just fell apart…* If only she *could* tell him how she felt. But that, Leslie knew, was impossible.

"Okay. Good. Well, how about this coming Saturday?"

"For the museum, you mean?"

"Yes."

She took a deep breath, remembering Sandi's words: *He doesn't really want to be just friends. And one of these days he's going to realize it. Don't you want to be there when he does?* "That sounds great."

The following Saturday dawned hot and muggy—a typical August day on the Gulf coast. Leslie riffled through her closet, looking for something flattering and cool to wear. She finally settled on a pale yellow cotton sundress and her brown leather sandals. She took great care with her makeup and hair, wanting to look her very best today.

She had a bad case of the butterflies. She hadn't seen Brian all week, and she'd missed him desperately.

At ten o'clock, as promised, he and Jeffrey arrived. A rush of warmth engulfed her as she watched Brian get out of the truck and walk up the front walk. He was dressed in gray Dockers and a wine knit shirt. His hair gleamed with gold highlights in the morning sunlight. Her hands trembled as she reached for her purse.

She knew she had to get a grip on herself, or he would take one look at her and know everything she was feeling. She took several deep breaths. *Calm down, calm down.* By the time he rang the doorbell, she had herself under some semblance of control.

"Hi," she said, opening the door.

He smiled. "Hi." His eyes swept her. "You look nice."

"Thanks." He looked nice, too, but she didn't trust herself to say it. The way she felt now, she just might throw herself into his arms and never let go.

So she just walked out and locked the door behind her.

"What did you do with Charlie today?" she asked Jeffrey once they were on their way.

"Edie's keeping him," he said.

The day turned out to be one of the nicest Leslie had ever spent. The museum was crowded, but not overly so, and after buying their IMAX tickets, they strolled through the main floor exhibits until it was time to see the movie.

The movie lived up to expectations. Leslie loved the whole IMAX experience, loved the feeling that she was actually in each of the airplanes, soaring among the clouds and over the Grand Canyon.

When it was over, Jeffrey said, "Awesome."

"I thought 'awesome' was out," Brian teased.

Jeffrey rolled his eyes. "Dad."

Brian laughed and winked at her, and Leslie's heart gave a little bounce.

Since it was too early for dinner, they decided to go back into the museum and see some of the exhibits they'd missed. It was six o'clock before Brian said, "I'm getting hungry. How about you two?"

They ate at one of the seafood restaurants on the Gulf Freeway, and it was close to nine o'clock before they got back to the island. Jeffrey had fallen asleep on the way home and didn't awaken, even when Brian pulled into Leslie's driveway and stopped the truck.

Leslie thought he might wake up when she got out, but he slept on.

As he always did, Brian walked her to the door. The porch was dark, and Brian held her arm as they climbed the steps. "You need some kind of lamp out here. You know, one that goes on automatically when it gets dark."

"I know. I guess I should turn on the porch light before I leave, but that seems like advertising that no one's home."

By now they'd reached the door, and Leslie fumbled for her key. She found it and squinted to find the lock.

"Here," Brian said, "let me." He reached for the keys and his hand closed around hers.

They both went still. Long seconds passed. His hand tightened around hers, slowly bringing her closer.

Leslie's heart went *thump, thump, thump.* She was afraid to breathe.

And then his arms went around her, and he pulled her to him. She could feel his heart beating against hers, and then he lowered his head and fitted his mouth to hers.

After the first stunned second, Leslie reacted instinctively, twining her arms around his neck and returning his kiss with all the pent-up need and love that had so long been denied.

And then, as suddenly as it began, the kiss ended. Leslie trembled; her knees felt weak. Brian leaned his forehead against hers, his breathing ragged. They stood that way a few seconds. Finally, he murmured,

"I'd better get back to the truck. I'll call you tomorrow."

Leslie was too shaken to speak, but she nodded.

He put his hand under her chin, lifting her face. "Leslie..."

In the darkness, her eyes searched his. "Yes?" she whispered.

"Nothing. We'll talk tomorrow."

Brian's mind spun as he drove home. He was thankful Jeffrey was still sleeping, because there was no way he could have carried on anything resembling rational conversation.

He still couldn't believe what he'd done.

One minute he'd had nothing more on his mind than helping her unlock her door.

The next all conscious thought disappeared and he was kissing her. He swallowed. That kiss. It had nearly been his undoing. He hadn't wanted to end it. Not only had he not wanted to end it, he'd wanted to sweep her up into his arms, take her inside, and make love to her until the sun came up.

The knowledge shook him. This was madness. In fact, the entire summer had been madness. He had been like a little kid, playing with fire, pretending that he could keep playing without getting burned. Telling himself that of course he and Leslie could be friends. Telling himself that the sexual attraction he felt for her was no big deal, he could live with it and not act on it. Telling himself all that was important was Jeffrey.

But now Brian knew he'd been lying to himself. Sure, Jeffrey's feelings were important. Very important. But so were his. And so were Leslie's. This situation wasn't fair to her. If they were to be friends only, Brian had to stick to his agreement, and tonight he certainly hadn't.

The question now was, what was he going to do next?

That night Leslie's dreams were filled with erotic images. She and Brian, lying in a darkened room, making love. Brian standing naked in the moonlight, his chiseled body as beautiful as a statue. Brian's hands touching her in all her secret places.

Several times she cried out.

She awakened in the middle of the night. Sitting up, she wrapped her arms around her knees and tried to still her trembling body.

She loved him so much.

What had the kiss meant? Was it possible he had changed his mind? That he loved her as she loved him? That he was ready to commit to her?

Because she knew she would never go back to sleep, she got up, went downstairs and made herself a cup of tea. Carrying it into the parlor, she curled up on the velvet chaise and slowly sipped it while she watched the play of moonlight across the hardwood floors.

He had said he would call her tomorrow.

She was afraid to find out why. Because after that kiss, if he still maintained that all he wanted from her was friendship, Leslie knew she wouldn't be able to bear it.

Leslie skipped church. She decided she would also skip dinner at her folks'. A little later, she'd call her mother and say she thought she might be coming down with a cold. Her mother wouldn't like it, but Leslie simply couldn't face her today.

To keep herself from going crazy thinking about Brian, she changed into a pair of old jeans and a paint-spattered shirt, then escaped to her studio upstairs where she spent the morning working on a watercolor of the Jean LaFitte Market. She'd taken photos and done the initial sketches weeks ago but hadn't had time to do the actual painting.

No wonder. She'd been spending so much of her free time with Brian and Jeffrey, she hadn't had time to do a great many of the things she used to do.

At eleven o'clock, she called her mother, who—just as Leslie had known—wasn't pleased when she said she wasn't coming for dinner.

"You don't take proper care of yourself," Peggy said. "It's no wonder you get sick all the time."

"I don't get sick all the time," Leslie said, pushing away the guilt she felt about lying.

"Are you going to work tomorrow?"

"I don't know. I'll see how I feel."

When they hung up, Leslie sighed.

She finished the painting a few minutes after twelve and cleaned up before heading downstairs.

Her stomach grumbled, and she realized she had forgotten to eat breakfast.

In the kitchen, she assembled the makings for a salad. Just as she was slicing a tomato, the phone rang.

Her heart skipped.

A bit shakily, she picked up the receiver. "Hello."

"Leslie?"

She put her hand over her heart, willing it to slow down. "Hi, Brian."

"You busy?"

She eyed the salad. "Um, no."

"I'd like to come over, if that's okay with you."

"Okay, sure. When did you want to come?"

"Well, there's a movie Jeffrey wants to see, and I'm going to go pick up his friend Scott, then drop the kids at the theater. I'll come after that, okay?"

"Okay. Have you had your lunch?"

"No."

"I'll fix you lunch, then."

When she hung up, she rooted through the pantry. Taking out a box of fettucine noodles, she decided she would make fettucine Alfredo to go with the salad.

Once she'd put the pasta on, she began making her sauce and tried not to think. But it was hard not to, because last night had marked a turning point in her relationship with Brian. The question was, which way would they go now?

It was nearly one o'clock by the time Brian arrived. The fettucine was ready and in a covered casserole in the microwave. The table was set, the salad ready and waiting in the refrigerator. Leslie just finished making a pitcher of iced tea when the doorbell rang.

It was only then she realized she hadn't changed clothes. Well, it was too late now. Besides, she didn't think a change of clothes was going to make any difference to Brian. He either loved her or he didn't.

She opened the door, took one look at his face and her heart sank. *Please, God…* But she was terribly afraid her prayer was futile.

"Hi," he said softly.

"Hi." She gave him a bright smile. "C'mon back to the kitchen. Lunch is ready." *No matter what he says, don't let him see you hurting. Hold yourself together until he's gone.*

"Have a seat," she said when they were in the kitchen. She headed for the refrigerator and the salad.

"Leslie, I'm sorry about last night."

She swallowed. Slowly took the salad out of the refrigerator, then finally turned to face him. "There's nothing to be sorry about."

"Yes, there is. We had a deal, and I didn't live up to it."

Fear caused her chest to constrict. She knew what was coming next.

"I don't think it's possible for us to keep seeing

each other and just be friends,'' he finished quietly. His eyes betrayed his distress.

Leslie was determined not to cry. Not to show by even a flicker of an eye that every word was like a knife plunging into her heart. If this was to be her last time with Brian, she would behave with dignity. She didn't want to make him feel any worse than he already did.

''I think you're right,'' she managed to say in almost a normal tone of voice. ''And Jeffrey? What will you tell him?''

''When he asks, I'll just say you're busy. And I hoped if by some chance he called you himself, you'd back me up.''

''Of course I will.''

The relief on Brian's face was another twist of the blade.

''Next weekend,'' he said, ''I thought I'd take Jeffrey and we'd go up to Canada—join his grandparents for a week or so. And then, when we get back, school will be starting. He'll be busy.''

Why don't you say it? He'll forget me. Leslie hadn't known it was possible to hurt this badly. It took all her strength to keep her face and voice composed. ''That sounds like a good plan.''

''I'm glad you understand.'' He shifted awkwardly. ''Look, maybe it's best if we just forget about lunch.''

Although she wanted nothing more than for him to go so she could give way to the misery churning inside, she couldn't. All she had left was her pride,

TRISHA ALEXANDER   215

and somehow she would hang onto it. "Don't be silly. Lunch is ready."

"Well..." He eyed the table.

"Please. Sit down. I'll just get the fettucine." She walked to the microwave, turning her back to him. She punched in numbers to heat the pasta, even though it didn't need heating. But she needed these few minutes to get herself under control, because she could feel the tears threatening. Oh, God. It would be awful to break down in front of Brian. She should have let him go home when he offered. What had she been thinking? That she was some kind of superwoman?

The microwave dinged. She opened it and removed the casserole, placing it on the stove. There was a lump in her throat the size of an orange. Her eyes filled. She knew she had to get away from him. "Excuse me for a moment," she said, rushing blindly from the room. She escaped into the half bath that connected with the TV room. Her hands were shaking as she covered her hot face.

A moment later, she felt his hand on her shoulder.

Gently, he turned her to face him. Leslie knew she was going to lose it. The tears overflowed, running down her face.

Brian's face twisted. "Oh, Leslie," he whispered.

And then she was in his arms.

He kissed her hungrily, his tongue tangling with hers. She could taste the salt of her tears along with the distinct flavor that was Brian. His hands slid under her shirt, touching the bare skin of her back.

"Leslie," he muttered against her mouth.

He kissed her again and again. She clung to him, all thought, all reason, gone in the passion raging between them.

When his hands moved down to cup her bottom and press her close, she moaned. She wanted him so much.

Later, she was never sure how they managed to get through the doorway into the TV room, but somehow they did. And the next thing she knew, they were lying together on the carpeted floor, and Brian was unzipping her jeans.

Chapter Twelve

There was no subtlety in their lovemaking. No playfulness. No finesse.

They wanted each other. It was a primal need, as old as time itself, and once that need was awakened, they couldn't wait.

One minute Brian was unzipping her jeans, the next their clothes were thrown anywhere they landed. The whole time they were undressing themselves and each other, Brian was kissing her and touching her.

Once their clothes were off, they tumbled to the floor.

It all happened so fast. There was no rational thought. Just a terrible hunger for each other that wouldn't be denied.

She gasped as he entered her, closing her eyes and holding on tightly as he pushed deeply inside. Almost immediately, spasms of intense pleasure rippled through her, and moments later he cried out, shuddering as his life force spilled into her.

Afterwards, they lay side by side as their hearts slowed and their bodies calmed. It was only then that the ramifications of her actions began to sink in.

Dear heaven, what had she done?

She was afraid to look at him. Afraid of what she might see in his eyes.

For agonizing moments, the only sounds in the room were their shallow breathing and the ticking of the wall clock. Finally, Brian spoke, his voice ragged, and she knew he was as upset as she was. "I never meant for this to happen."

The look in his eyes made her want to cry. Oh, God. Did he think she *had?* Did he think she had somehow *planned* this? Horrified, she sat up and reached for her shirt. Suddenly all she wanted to do was cover herself.

Silent now, he stood. Even as upset as she was, she couldn't help noticing how beautiful his body was. She ached with love for him. If only he would say something tender. Something to show he wasn't blaming her. Something to show their lovemaking, even though it was unplanned and unwise, had meant something to him.

But he said nothing. Avoiding her eyes, he began to dress. She felt numb, frozen, as she watched him.

When he'd finished dressing, he finally looked at her. The regret on his face hurt more than a physical blow.

"I'm sorry," he said. "I have to go. Jeffrey will be waiting for me."

"It's okay," she managed to answer, even though her heart was splintering. "Go."

The moment she heard the front door close behind him, she burst into tears.

Brian drove aimlessly. His emotions were chaotic. What had he done? He was furious with himself. He had gone to Leslie's to tell her he couldn't see her again and ended up making love to her. Was he crazy?

He felt stunned, as if he'd been in a knockout fight. His actions today had been totally unlike him. Yet the moment he'd seen those tears shimmering in Leslie's eyes, he had been powerless to stop himself. What began as the need to comfort her was almost immediately ignited into full-flamed desire. From then on, he hadn't thought at all.

Brian rarely swore, but now he hit the steering wheel and let loose with a string of curses. He was disgusted with himself. Today he had acted like a randy teenager and done something stupid and reckless, without a thought to the consequences.

He hadn't even used a condom! What if he'd gotten Leslie pregnant? After all, she'd never said she couldn't get pregnant. She'd said she had miscarried.

He couldn't imagine what she was thinking now. He wouldn't blame her if she hated him, especially after the way he'd left her. That, above all else, made him feel ashamed of himself. He'd known she was as upset as he was, that she, too, had been swept along by the emotion of the moment, and he should have said something comforting. Something to let her know he didn't blame her, that he blamed himself.

Once more, he hit the steering wheel, this time so hard he hurt his hand. Because losing control of himself and making love to Leslie was not the worst thing he had done today. Oh, no. The worst thing he had done was leave her in such an ungentlemanlike way. Shame nearly overwhelmed him.

He knew he had to get a grip on himself, because the movie would be over soon. And since Joy's death, Jeffrey had become sensitive to Brian's moods. He would be bound to know that something was wrong if Brian was still upset when he arrived at the theater.

If only Brian knew what to do now.

Think about this later. Go get Jeffrey, and tonight, after he's in bed, when you're calmer and can think straighter, you can decide on a course of action.

He knew this was sensible, so he made an effort to wipe his mind clean and headed toward the theater. The movie was letting out just as Brian pulled into the pickup zone. He parked, and a few minutes later saw Jeffrey and Scott emerge. He honked, and they raced toward the truck.

"How was the movie?" he said when they'd clambered in.

"Great!" said Jeffrey.

"Awesome!" said Scott.

They talked excitedly about the adventure saga all the way to Scott's house, and Brian was grateful for their chatter.

"I'll bet Charlie missed me," Jeffrey said when they'd dropped off Scott and were headed toward home.

"I'll bet he did, too."

Brian had put the puppy in the utility room when he left. Charlie was house-trained now and could have been left alone a couple of hours without incident, but he liked to chew. Jeffrey had balked the first time Brian banished the puppy, but Brian had been firm.

"Charlie will outgrow the chewing," he'd said. "Then he won't have to be shut up." He hoped this was true.

Jeffrey continued to chatter, and before long they were pulling into their subdivision. As the Suburban crested the small rise leading to their street, Brian frowned. There was a car parked in their driveway.

Then, as realization struck, his heart slammed against his chest. It was a gold Lexus. Hank's car!

What were Jeffrey's grandparents doing there now? They weren't supposed to come home from Canada for two and a half more weeks.

As he drove closer, he could see Hank and Theresa sitting on the deck. Had they come home be-

cause they suspected something? Brian was so con-
sumed with guilt he was sure Hank and Theresa
would immediately know what he had been doing
just an hour and a half earlier.

Hank waved. He and Theresa got up.

Brian waved back, saying, "Jeffrey, look, it's
Grandma and Grandpa," as his mind whirled.

"Grandma and Grandpa!" Jeffrey shouted.

Brian pulled into the driveway, and before he and
Jeffrey were even out of the truck, Hank and Theresa were there.

Jeffrey catapulted himself into his grandmother's
arms. Brian and Hank watched, smiling as Theresa
bestowed at least a dozen kisses on Jeffrey, who
pretended not to like it but did. "Oh, I missed you
so much," she said. "Why, you've grown two
inches this summer."

"What made you come home early?" Brian said
to Hank.

"It was me. I was homesick for you and Jeffrey,"
Theresa said, walking over to give Brian a hug, too.
"I kept thinking of you both, and something told
me we just had to come home."

Brian felt sick with guilt.

"We haven't even been to the house yet," Hank
said. "She insisted on coming here first. She
couldn't wait to see you."

"Have you been waiting long?"

"Only about twenty minutes," Hank answered.

"Where were you?" Theresa asked.

"Scott and me went to see *The Eliminator*," Jeffrey said.

Theresa frowned. *"The Eliminator?"*

"Yeah, it's this cool movie about this space guy who comes to earth and saves the world from these aliens. You should have seen it, Grandma! It was great!"

Theresa smiled and ruffled Jeffrey's hair.

"Grandma, Grandpa, don't you want to see Charlie?" Jeffrey said.

"Oh, that's right," Hank said. "Your dog."

"C'mon, let's go inside. Gimme the keys, Dad. I'll unlock the door."

Brian handed Jeffrey the keys, and he took off. By the time they entered the kitchen, he had released Charlie from the utility room, and the puppy raced around in circles, barking the whole time.

Hank laughed.

Theresa said, "My, he's boisterous, isn't he?"

"That's putting it mildly," Brian said.

"Isn't he great?" Jeffrey said, scooping up Charlie and doing his best to hold on to the wiggling pup.

Hank and Theresa petted the dog and made all the appropriate admiring remarks, while Brian struggled to get his turbulent emotions under control. He wondered how long the Paladinos would stay. If they hadn't even been home yet, they probably wouldn't stay long. He hoped not. He wasn't up to any kind of close scrutiny from them. He needed some time and distance from today's events.

They stayed about an hour, and somehow Brian got through it without betraying himself, even when Theresa asked Jeffrey to tell her everything he'd done since they last talked. Brian held his breath, sure Jeffrey would say something about Leslie. But he didn't. He started to, then Hank noticed Charlie chewing on the leg of a chair, and in the commotion that followed, the subject was changed, and Brian breathed a sigh of relief.

A little after four, Hank said, "I think we should be getting on home, Theresa. Get the car unpacked and everything."

"Oh, I know, you're antsy," she said, getting up. "Okay, I'm ready. Jeffrey, do you want to come with us?"

"Can I bring Charlie?"

"Sure," Hank said, "but he'll have to go in the backyard."

"That's okay. He likes backyards. He plays—"

"When you get outside, you'd better make sure he goes before you get in the car," Brian interrupted before Jeffrey could say anything about Leslie's backyard, which he was sure he'd been about to.

"I know, Dad."

"Give me a call when you're ready to come home," Brian said. "I'll come and get you."

"Instead, how about if we all have dinner together tonight?" Hank said. "I know Theresa won't feel like cooking."

"Even if I did, there's no food in the house," she

said. "In fact, we'd better stop at the store on the way home. At least to get some bread and milk."

"So what do you think?" Hank said. "Do you want to come by about six?"

Brian didn't want to say yes, but he didn't see how he could refuse. "All right. Where do you want to go?"

"Well, I haven't had Mexican food since we left," Hank said.

"Let's go to Pepé's, then," Theresa said, smiling. "I love their tamales."

"Okay. Sounds good."

"Let's ask Leslie to go, too," Jeffrey said.

Theresa's smile faded.

"No, Jeffrey," Brian said firmly, hoping his face didn't betray the chaos inside him. "Tonight is family."

Jeffrey frowned. "But, Dad—"

"Jeffrey," Brian warned. "I said no."

Jeffrey subsided into sullen silence.

Hank said soothingly, "Your friend can come with us another time, Jeffrey. Grandma and I don't want to share you tonight."

Jeffrey sighed. "Okay."

It was another ten minutes or so before they left. Once they were gone, Brian knew what he had to do.

He picked up the phone and punched in Leslie's number. It rang four times, then the answering machine clicked on.

Hi. This is Leslie. At the tone, leave a message.

When the beep sounded, he said, "Leslie? It's Brian. If you're there, please pick up. I have to talk to you."

There was a click, then another beep, then her voice. "Hello, Brian." She sounded distant, her tone expressionless. "What can I do for you?"

He closed his eyes.

He had never felt like such a heel.

"Leslie, something has happened." He quickly explained about the Paladinos. "I had intended to try to come over tonight. I know we have to talk."

"What's there to talk about?" she said in a flat voice. "Everything's already been said. Have a good life, Brian."

"But Leslie, we can't just—"

But she had hung up.

Brian felt sick. Today he had acted without thinking, and in the process, he had hurt a fine person, someone who didn't deserve this kind of treatment.

He looked at the dead receiver. Should he call her back? She probably wouldn't answer. Should he go over there? And then what? What could he possibly say to make things better?

No. Going over there, trying to apologize and explain, might make *him* feel better, but it would do nothing for her. This was best. She hated him, and he deserved it.

End of story.

Leslie sat by the phone for a long time. If she'd harbored even the slightest hope that the lovemaking she and Brian had shared would make a difference to him, that phone call had shattered it.

He didn't love her.

He had made love to her because he felt sorry for her. And because he was human and she was willing. Her face flamed as she remembered just how willing. She'd practically thrown herself at him.

She buried her face in her hands.

She wished she could just disappear from the face of the earth.

The evening was agonizing for Brian. He tried not to think, but the day's events refused to go away. It was all he could do to pretend things were normal and to carry on a conversation with Hank and Theresa. But mostly, he worried that Jeffrey might bring up Leslie's name again, and he knew he couldn't handle questions about her tonight. But the evening passed without her name coming up again. Still, he was exhausted from the stress and couldn't wait to go home where he could finally relax.

"You look tired," Theresa said while they waited for the bill. "Have you been working hard?"

"You know what summer's like," Brian said evasively.

She nodded, but her eyes were thoughtful, and Brian was sure she suspected something.

Finally, it was time to leave. Brian drove the Paladinos home, where Jeffrey collected Charlie.

"Tomorrow night," Theresa said, "I want you two to come *here* for dinner. We'll have a belated birthday celebration for Jeffrey. A cake and every-thing.''

Jeffrey grinned happily.

Everyone hugged and said good-night.

As Brian drove home, he felt drained. But he knew he couldn't relax long. It might not have hap-pened tonight and it might not happen tomorrow, but the subject of Leslie would not be postponed forever. And when it *did* come up, he'd better be prepared with answers.

Leslie cried herself to sleep. And the next day she did something she hadn't done in years. She called in sick. Then she crawled back into bed and buried herself under the covers.

When she finally got up, it was past noon. She took one look at herself in the mirror and cringed. She looked awful. Worse than awful. She looked like a witch.

''All right,'' she said aloud. ''It's time to stop feeling sorry for yourself. So you made a fool of yourself over a man. So you had sex with him and then he walked out. So what? It's not death and it's not world peace.''

After a shower, two Advil, and a cup of fresh coffee, she actually felt better. For the rest of the day she determinedly kept thoughts of Brian out of her mind by spending the time in her studio, paint-ing.

She knew this was only a temporary reprieve. She

could always lose herself in her painting, but tomorrow she would have to face the real world again.

A world without Brian.

She took a deep breath. She wanted to cry again, but she wouldn't let herself. Tears solved nothing. She had learned that lesson a long time ago.

What *did* help was finding something else to focus on, and to that end, she would spend her energy and her emotion on preparing for the child she hoped would soon be hers.

The week was terrible for Brian. He couldn't stop thinking about Leslie. At home. At the office. In the car. Out in the field. Wherever he was, whatever he was doing, thoughts of her would intrude.

He kept thinking about what it had felt like to make love to her. And what it would feel like to *really* make love to her. Slowly. In a real bed. Without guilt.

He knew he had to stop thinking this way, because it wasn't going to happen. Even if, somehow, Hank and Theresa gave their blessing, Brian knew Leslie probably never wanted to speak to him again.

He told himself to forget about her. Whatever might have been between them was lost. But it was hard to follow his own advice. For one thing, even if he *had* managed to put her out of his mind, she wouldn't stay out long, because Jeffrey couldn't stop talking about her. He kept asking why they couldn't have her over and why they couldn't go to her house.

Worse, twice he mentioned her name in the presence of his grandparents. The second time, they were at the Paladinos. Later, Hank drew Brian aside.

"Tell me the truth," he said. "Is this woman just someone Jeffrey likes, or are you interested in her?"

Brian had never lied to Hank, and he didn't want to start now. He hedged. "Would it bother you if I was?"

The older man's shoulders sagged. "I know it's wrong of Theresa and I to feel this way, Brian, but yes, it would. I know that you're young, and someday you'll probably want to marry again. But right now, it's…it's just too soon."

Brian couldn't fault Hank for his feelings. He knew how his father-in-law had felt about Joy, how he and Theresa had adored her. Her death had nearly destroyed them. In fact, if it hadn't been for Jeffrey, Brian was sure neither one would have had the will to go on. He put his hand on Hank's shoulder.

"Don't worry, Hank," he said. "Like you said, maybe someday, but right now, I'm not ready to get involved with anyone else." He told himself he had spoken the truth, but if that was so, why did he suddenly feel so bereft?

Later that night, as Jeffrey was getting ready for bed, he said, "Dad, can I ask you something?"

"Of course."

"Doesn't Leslie like us anymore?"

Brian had known some form of this question was bound to come up sooner or later, so he wasn't caught completely off guard. Even so, there was an ache in his chest when he answered. "Of course she likes us. She's just been busy lately, that's all." He hated himself when he saw the bleak look in Jeffrey's eyes.

I'll make it up to him, he vowed. *I don't know how, but somehow I'll make it up to him.*

Despite Leslie's lecture to herself on Monday, she had a hard time getting through the week. She knew she had to snap out of her blue funk, and soon. Sunday was her parents' forty-fifth wedding anniversary, and Michelle and Nick were having a dinner party for them at their home. Leslie was dreading it.

She missed Brian and Jeffrey so much. The missing was an actual physical pain. She knew that as time passed, the pain would lessen. It had to. No one could live with this kind of hurt forever.

She felt terrible that she hadn't had a chance to at least talk to Jeffrey. She wondered what he must think. She wondered what Brian had told him. She wished she at least knew if Jeffrey was okay.

On Sunday, as she was dressing for the party, the phone rang. In the midst of applying her makeup, she decided to let the answering machine pick up, but she walked over to her bedside table and listened.

"This is Jeffrey. I just wanted to—"

She grabbed the receiver. "Jeffrey?"

"Oh, hi, Leslie. You're home."

"Yes, I am. I'm so glad to hear from you."

"Are you?" He sounded uncertain.

"Yes, of course."

"Dad says you're busy, that's why you can't do stuff with us."

Oh, God. "I *have* been awfully busy, Jeffrey, but you know, you're going back to school soon, and your Dad says your grandparents are home now, so you're busy, too."

"I'd never be too busy to see you," Jeffrey said sadly.

Leslie swallowed against the lump in her throat. "Oh, Jeffrey, what a nice thing to say."

After a few seconds, he said hopefully, "But you're not busy tonight, are you? I could tell Dad, and maybe we could do something together like we used to."

"Honey, I wish I could, but I *am* busy tonight. It's my parents' anniversary and I'm getting ready to go to a party for them."

"Oh."

Leslie wanted to cry. She couldn't even say, *Maybe another time.* She took a deep breath. "I have to go now, Jeffrey. Thanks for calling. It was wonderful to hear from you."

After they'd hung up, Leslie decided life could be so unfair. She wished she could think of something to do to make things easier for Jeffrey, but there was nothing.

Eventually, he'll forget about me.

The thought brought her no comfort.

Chapter Thirteen

"What's wrong, Leslie?"

Leslie looked at her sister-in-law. The two of them were alone in the kitchen for the first time that evening.

"I know something is," Michelle said kindly. "Want to talk about it?"

Leslie sighed, then nodded. "Yes, I do. But let's go outside, okay? I don't want anyone, especially Mom, to walk in on us."

Michelle took off her apron, and they headed out back. The turquoise water of the kidney-shaped pool, which took up the better part of the yard, sparkled from the underwater lights. Michelle headed for the far corner of the yard, where a raised deck was flanked by azalea and crepe myrtle bushes.

They sat on one of the wooden benches that were built into the deck. The night was filled with sounds: the whir of the pool filter, the drone of an airplane overhead, the buzzing of cicadas, and from somewhere down the block, the deep bark of a dog.

"Okay, tell me," Michelle said, crossing her legs and leaning forward. In the moonlight, her pale pink chiffon dress looked silvery as it settled around her.

Leslie told her everything. Thankfully, when she was finished, Michelle didn't preach or lecture. She just moved closer and put her arms around Leslie and hugged her.

"I understand exactly how you feel," she said, "because something similar happened to me before I met Nick."

"It did?"

Michelle nodded. "I'm not proud of it, because the man in question was really a jerk, and I don't think Brian is."

"No," Leslie said. "He's not."

"I wish I knew what to tell you," Michelle said.

Leslie shrugged. "I know you don't have magic answers. I don't expect any. It just feels good to unburden myself."

Just then, the back door opened, and Nick walked out. "Hey, what're you two doing out there?" he called.

"Just talking," Michelle said. "We'll be in soon."

He shut the door and walked closer. "Mom's looking for you."

"Oh, oh," Leslie said. "We'd better go in." The last thing she needed was her mother's curiosity aroused. She stood.

Michelle got up, too. Softly, so Nick couldn't hear, she said, "Anytime you need a shoulder, I'll be here."

Leslie smiled gratefully.

That night, for the first time since Brian had walked out of her house that fateful Sunday, Leslie slept without dreaming about him.

And the next morning, as she got ready for work, she told herself that even though she would probably always love him, she would survive.

Sunday night and all day Monday, Brian thought about Jeffrey. Because although Jeffrey didn't know it, Brian had overheard his conversation with Leslie. He'd been downstairs reading and remembered that one of his neighbors had asked him for the number of his accountant.

So Brian got up and walked out to the kitchen, which was where he kept his Rolodex. He looked up the number for the accountant, lifted the receiver...and heard Leslie's voice.

He very nearly dropped the phone. He almost said something.

And then he heard Jeffrey's voice. Brian knew it was wrong to listen, but he couldn't seem to stop himself.

Jeffrey was saying, "Dad says you're busy, that's why you can't do stuff with us."

Then Leslie had answered, "I *have* been awfully busy, Jeffrey, but you know, you're going back to school soon, and your dad says your grandparents are home now, so you're busy, too."

"I'd never be too busy to see you." It hurt Brian to hear the sadness in his son's voice.

"Oh, Jeffrey, what a nice thing to say," Leslie had said.

A few seconds went by. Brian held his breath, afraid they might hear him.

Then Jeffrey had said, his voice filled with hope, "But you're not busy tonight, are you? I could tell Dad, and maybe we could do something together like we used to."

"Honey, I wish I could, but I *am* busy tonight," she answered. "It's my parents' anniversary and I'm getting ready to go to a party for them."

"Oh." There was a world of dejection in that one word.

Leslie had said softly, "I have to go now, Jeffrey. Thanks for calling. It was wonderful to hear from you."

When Brian heard Jeffrey hang up, he hung up, too. Afterward, he stood there for a long time. And ever since, he hadn't been able to think about anything else.

It wasn't fair to Jeffrey to let him go on thinking the reason they hadn't seen Leslie was because she was too busy for them. Nor was it fair to her to have asked her to lie.

But how could he tell Jeffrey the truth?

By the time Brian left the office to go home Monday night, he'd come to a decision. He would talk to Jeffrey tonight. Although he couldn't tell Jeffrey the whole truth, because the boy was too young to understand, he could tell him enough of the truth to make him feel better.

Edie was bustling about the kitchen when Brian walked in. "Hi, Mr. Canfield," she said, giving him a big smile.

"Hello, Edie." Her tote bag was sitting on the kitchen table, which meant she was in a hurry to leave tonight.

"Jeffrey's upstairs doing his homework." She turned the gas down low under a covered pot. "This here's red beans and rice with some nice smoked sausage cut up in it, and there's a salad in the refrigerator."

"Thanks. Sounds good."

She picked up her tote. "I'm gonna be off, then. I have my bunco tonight."

"Have fun."

"I always do!"

After she left, Brian debated calling Jeffrey downstairs to talk to him, but decided to wait until dinner.

An hour later, with just a few bites left on Jeffrey's plate, Brian said, "You feeling okay, son?"

Jeffrey shrugged. "Sure, Dad. Why?"

"Well, to tell the truth, I overheard your conversation with Leslie yesterday."

Jeffrey stared at him.

"I know it's not right to eavesdrop, but I couldn't

help it,'' Brian continued. ''I know you feel bad about not seeing her and I wanted to try to explain to you what's going on.'' He waited, wishing Jeffrey would say something instead of looking at him as if he were some kind of criminal. ''See, the thing is, sometimes it's hard for men and women to be friends. Things happen, and…'' Brian sighed. ''This is going to be hard for you to understand, but I'm going to try—''

''I don't understand anything!'' Jeffrey blurted out. ''I thought you and Leslie were gonna get married!'' Then he jumped up, knocking over his chair in the process, and ran out of the room and up the stairs.

But not before Brian had seen the tears in his eyes.

Brian sat out on the deck almost the entire night. He thought about Jeffrey and what he'd said. He thought about Leslie. He thought about Hank and Theresa. He thought about Joy.

And finally, he thought about himself.

As the first light of dawn stained the morning sky, he finally admitted he loved Leslie.

The knowledge freed something in him, and he felt lighter than he had in days. In weeks. And, no matter what the consequences, he knew what he had to do.

Later, after Edie arrived and Jeffrey had gone to school, Brian called Brenda and told her he would not be in until later that afternoon.

"I've got something important I must take care of."

"Okay, see you later."

His first stop was the bank, his second was the jewelry store where he knew the owner, his third was the florist's. Then, armed with the ring he'd purchased and a dozen yellow roses, he headed for Dr. Singer's office.

Leslie had decided to start on the August accounts receivable that morning. She had just brought up the spread sheet on her computer when the bell announcing a visitor tinkled.

She looked up, and her heart nearly stopped.

At first she thought she was dreaming.

It couldn't be Brian standing there. It must be a mirage.

Then the mirage moved.

It was only then she noticed the bouquet of yellow roses in his arms. Her heart began to pound. What did this mean?

He slowly walked forward, his eyes never leaving hers. Carefully, he set the roses down on her desk. Then he walked around to where she sat, frozen and stunned. Reaching down, he took her hands and pulled her up, then folded her into his arms.

She couldn't have spoken if her life depended on it. He kissed her then—a long, tender, breath-stealing kiss that made her heart soar.

"I love you, Leslie," he said as the kiss finally

ended. "And I want to marry you! Can you forgive me for being so stupid, and will you be my wife?"

Leslie's eyes filled with tears. She could hardly believe this was happening. "Oh, Brian. I love you, too. I think I've loved you from the first day I saw you."

"Really?"

"Yes, really."

"So you forgive me?"

"Yes, I forgive you."

"And you'll marry me?"

"Yes, I'll marry you."

He held her close. "We may have some rough patches ahead," he murmured against her forehead.

Leslie knew he was thinking of Joy's parents. "I know." Wait'll he met *her* mother. The thought caused her to smile.

"I almost forgot." Drawing back a little, he reached into his pocket and pulled out a small black velvet box. When he opened it, she gasped in delight. The ring was a gorgeous round solitaire diamond set in platinum. Her hand trembled as he raised it and slipped the ring on her left hand.

"It's loose, isn't it?" he said.

"Yes, a little."

"We can fix that. Do you like it?"

"Oh, Brian. I love it. It's the most beautiful ring I've ever seen."

She threw her arms around him, and they were in the middle of another long, wonderful kiss when her intercom buzzed. Guiltily, they jumped apart, and

Leslie laughed. "That's Dr. Singer," she said. "I'd better go see what he wants."

"All right. You go take care of your boss, and I'll get to work myself. But tonight, I want you to come to my house after work, okay? I want us to tell Jeffrey together."

Leslie practically floated into Dr. Singer's office. He took one look at her face and said, "What's got you looking so happy?"

Unable to stop smiling, she held out her hand.

"Well, well," he said. "What's this?"

"It's an engagement ring."

"I figured that. And who's the lucky man?"

"Brian Canfield."

Dr. Singer didn't say anything for so long, Leslie began to feel uneasy. Just as she was about to ask him if something was wrong, he grinned. "I guess I should have suspected, but I didn't. All I have to say is, Brian Canfield is one lucky fellow."

"You're getting married?" Jeffrey squealed. His eyes were two saucers. "Really?"

Leslie and Brian answered in unison. "Really."

"And you're really gonna be my mother, Leslie?"

For a moment, Leslie was afraid Brian would be upset. But he smiled at her, and if there was a hint of sadness in his eyes, she understood.

"I know I can never take the place of your real mother," Leslie answered gently, "but I will be honored to be your stepmother."

"Cool," Jeffrey said.

After that, the three of them hugged and laughed and talked about the future. Several times, Leslie wanted to pinch herself to make sure all of this was true and really happening and not some dream.

But it wasn't a dream. Her prayers had all been answered. She finally had the family she'd always wanted.

Much later, after Jeffrey was in bed, and Brian and Leslie were sitting out on the deck, Brian said, "Tomorrow I'll go over and talk to Jeffrey's grandparents."

"How do you think they'll take the news?" Leslie asked.

Brian shook his head. "I don't know." A few seconds passed. "That's not completely true. I...think they'll be upset."

"I'm sorry," Leslie said softly.

He sighed. "Can't be helped. The last thing I want to do is hurt them, but last night I realized that even though they are very important to me, you and Jeffrey are more important. I love you and Jeffrey loves you and we're going to be married, and hard as it may be for them, they'll just have to accept that."

It was even harder than Brian had imagined it would be to tell the Paladinos. But somehow he got the words out. "I know this is a shock," he finished, "and that it will be hard for you at first, but Leslie's a wonderful woman, and I think you'll like her once you get to know her." He looked at the two of them hopefully.

For several moments, there was complete silence. Then Theresa's face crumpled and she began to cry. "How could you forget Joy so soon?"

Hank put his arms around her. He didn't say anything, just patted her, but his gaze met Brian's over her bowed head, and the look in his eyes was painful for Brian to see.

"I haven't forgotten Joy," Brian said, stung by her accusation, even as he understood why she'd made it. "I'll never forget her. But Joy is gone, and I don't want to live the rest of my life alone. Please try to understand."

In answer, Theresa only cried harder.

"I think it might be best if you left now," Hank said.

Brian started to say something else, then stopped. They needed time to digest his news. Time to work through the hurt. They were reasonable people. They were also kind and loving people. They would come around eventually.

"All right," he said. "We'll talk again when Theresa's not so upset." He walked over and squeezed Hank's shoulder. "I'm sorry."

Hank nodded.

As Brian walked out, he wondered why life was so complicated. He also wondered if he would ever again have the same relationship with the Paladinos as he'd had before today. He hoped so. He wouldn't want to lose their love and respect. But if he had to choose between them and Leslie, there would be no contest. It might have taken him some time to figure out what she meant to him, but he knew now. And nothing in the world would keep them apart from now on.

Four months later

"Sweetheart, have you seen my red tie?"

Leslie finished sprinkling green candy glitter on the last of the cookies she had baked to take to her parents' home for their traditional Christmas Eve dinner, then walked to the foot of the stairs. "Brian? I think I saw it draped over the back of the rocker," she called out. "Do you see it?"

A minute later, a sheepish-faced Brian appeared at the top of the stairs. "Yeah. Here it is." He held out the tie.

It constantly amazed Leslie that she still felt that rush of happiness every time she saw her husband after an absence, even if the absence was only half an hour. She smiled up at him. "You almost ready?"

"Yep."

"What about Jeffrey?"

"I'll check on him."

"Good, because I don't want to be late."

"We won't be late. Besides, you're not even dressed yet."

"It'll only take me a minute to put my dress on." Leslie hadn't wanted to wear her new forest green

velvet dress while she iced and decorated the cookies, so although her hair was fixed and her makeup
was on, she wore a robe over her slip.

"And it'll only take me half a minute to get it off
you later," he said in that teasing, sexy tone that
always made her knees feel weak.

"Promises, promises," Leslie said.

As she walked back to the kitchen, she thought
about how happy she was. She hadn't known it was
possible to be this happy. And in a few days, she
would be even happier, because yesterday she'd had
a call from Mrs. Wong. They had a little girl for her
and Brian. A five-year-old named Sarah. Leslie was
speechless at the news. She'd had no idea a child
would be available so soon.

"You still want to adopt a child, don't you?"
Mrs. Wong said, misinterpreting Leslie's silence.
"You haven't changed your minds?"

"Oh, no," Leslie said. "My husband and I want
another child very much."

When she told Brian, he hugged her fiercely.
"Our cup runneth over," he said.

Except for one thing. The Paladinos had never
accepted Leslie. When she and Brian were married
at the end of September, neither Hank nor Theresa
came to the wedding. For a while, it had been touch
and go as to whether Leslie's mother would be there,
either, but at the last minute, she gave in and came.

And gradually, as she had come to know Brian,
she had given him her grudging approval.

Bless Brian, Leslie thought. He had never said a

word about her mother. Not one criticism, even though Leslie was sure there was plenty he wanted to say.

He had given her so much. And he'd given *up* so much. He'd sold his beach home, even though he'd built it and Joy had decorated it and it contained so many memories, because he knew it wouldn't be fair of him to expect Leslie to live there. Leslie would always be grateful to him for that thoughtfulness, because as much as she loved him, she didn't think she would have been able to stand being reminded of Joy in every corner.

They lived in Leslie's house now, much to Jeffrey's delight.

But the most important thing he'd given up was his loving and close relationship with the Paladinos. He still saw them, but it wasn't the same. Theresa refused to set foot in their home, so he took Jeffrey there and picked him up. Leslie was certain he visited there sometimes, too, but he never talked about the visits.

She sighed.

She guessed a person couldn't have everything. In an ideal world, perhaps, the Paladinos would have been able to put aside their grief and disappointment and think of Brian's and Jeffrey's happiness. But it wasn't an ideal world.

Still, it was Christmas, and she knew they must be hurting. She wished she could think of a way to reconcile the family, because she knew Brian was saddened by the rift.

She began to put the decorated cookies on a crystal platter. As soon as she finished her task, she would go upstairs and put on the new dress.

And who knew? Tomorrow was Christmas, the day of miracles. Maybe somehow a miracle would happen for them.

The phone rang just as Brian was ready to walk downstairs. "I'll get it," he called, knowing Leslie was busy in the kitchen.

It was Hank. "Hello, Brian. Merry Christmas."

"Merry Christmas to you, Hank."

"Theresa wants to speak to Jeffrey. Is he there?"

"Sure. Let me get him."

Brian walked over to Jeffrey's room and knocked on the door. "Grandma's on the phone, Jeffrey."

The door opened and Jeffrey, who was in the middle of buttoning his new blue dress shirt, walked out. His hair was slicked down, but as he walked past, Brian noticed the part was uneven. He couldn't help smiling.

Jeffrey disappeared into the master bedroom, and Brian couldn't resist standing there a bit longer to listen to the conversation.

"Hi, Grandma. Merry Christmas."

There was silence for a while, then, "I can't, Grandma. Me and Dad and Leslie are going over to Grandma Marlowe's house tonight." More silence. Then Jeffrey said, "I know she's not my real grandmother and Leslie's not my mother, but Grandma,

Mom sent Leslie to us 'cause she knew I needed a mother and Dad needed somebody to love.''

With his son's words echoing in his mind, Brian quietly walked downstairs.

Later that night, after he and Leslie had made love, they lay together spoon fashion in their big bed and Brian idly caressed one of her small perfect breasts. She sighed happily, and he kissed her neck. He loved kissing her. He loved touching her. And he loved making her happy.

She was such a wonderful woman, and he was such a lucky man. Some men never find this kind of love, he thought in wonder, and I've found it twice. "Sweetheart, there's something I want to tell you.''

"Hmm?'' she said lazily.

He repeated what he'd overheard Jeffrey say to his grandmother Paladino.

For the longest time after he was finished, Leslie said nothing. And then he realized she was crying.

"Leslie, what is it? I thought knowing what Jeffrey said would make you happy.''

"It did. It does. But it also makes me sad, because I want Joy's parents to be happy, too.'' She twisted in his arms so they were facing each other. "I hate this terrible business between you and knowing I'm the cause of it.''

"You're not the cause of it,'' he said fiercely. "This business, as you call it, is the choice of Hank and Theresa. And it can be mended anytime they choose.''

The next morning, while Leslie and Brian and Jeffrey were opening their Christmas gifts, the doorbell rang.

Brian and Leslie looked at each other curiously.

Jeffrey, followed by Charlie, raced to the front door and yanked it open.

''Grandma! Grandpa!'' he shouted joyously.

Brian stood. He looked as stunned as Leslie felt. She got up, and together, they walked into the foyer. There stood the Paladinos, their arms filled with gifts, their faces uncertain.

''I'm sorry, Brian,'' Theresa said, her eyes filling with tears. Her eyes turned to Leslie. ''I was wrong, Leslie. Can you forgive me?''

And sometimes a little child shall lead them... Leslie thought, her heart filled to bursting. ''There's nothing to forgive,'' she said, smiling and opening her arms. After only a moment's hesitation, Theresa walked into her embrace.

As they hugged, Leslie's eyes met Brian's over Theresa's shoulder. And she knew he was feeling the same sense of wonder and thankfulness she was feeling, for now their family was really complete.

She had her Christmas miracle.

* * * * *

SILHOUETTE
SPECIAL EDITION
COMING NEXT MONTH

OPERATION: BABY Barbara Bretton

That's My Baby!

A brush with death can have a dramatic effect on your hormones…as Samantha Wilde and Duncan Stewart discover. A plane crash throws these strangers together—and three months later Sam finds out she's pregnant!

THE WINNING HAND Nora Roberts

The MacGregors

Darcy Wallace goes from being a pauper to a millionaire in a minute—and runs into seductive Robert MacGregor Blade. He's not the marrying kind, but Darcy's on a lucky streak—maybe she can win him, too!

A FAMILY KIND OF GIRL Lisa Jackson

Widowed Tiffany Santini tells her powerful brother-in-law J.D. that she's fine on her own. But when he showers her kids with affection, she realizes how much she wishes some of those kisses were for her!

FROM HOUSE CALLS TO HUSBAND Christine Flynn

Prescription: Marriage

Nurse Katie Sheppard has vowed never to marry a doctor, least of all handsome surgeon, Mike Brennan. Mike is her best friend, but lately she can't help noticing he's also great husband material…

PRENUPTIAL AGREEMENT Doris Rangel

Yance Chisolm doesn't know that China Smith has loved him for years, and when he proposes marriage it is for purely practical reasons. But he soon regrets their agreement *not* to share a bed…

AKA: MARRIAGE Jule McBride

Big Apple Babies

For years, ex-cop Shane Holiday has been haunted by an unsolved crime. He knows Lillian Smith is the key to the mystery, and so he goes undercover and makes her an offer she can't refuse—marriage!

COMING NEXT MONTH FROM
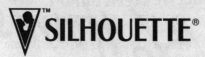
SILHOUETTE®

Intrigue
Danger, deception and desire

SOMEBODY'S BABY Amanda Stevens
SPENCER'S SECRET Laura Gordon
THE MISSING HOUR Dawn Stewardson
MYSTERY DAD Leona Karr

Desire
Provocative, sensual love stories

SLOW-TALKING TEXAN Mary Lynn Baxter
DEDICATED TO DEIRDRE Anne Marie Winston
THE CONSUMMATE COWBOY Sara Orwig
THE NON-COMMISSIONED BABY Maureen Child
COWBOYS DO IT BEST Eileen Wilks
THE TEXAS RANGER AND THE TEMPTING TWIN
Pamela Ingrahm

Sensation
A thrilling mix of passion, adventure and drama

THE BADDEST BRIDE IN TEXAS Maggie Shayne
MURPHY'S LAW Marilyn Pappano
EVERYDAY, AVERAGE JONES Suzanne Brockmann
ONE MORE KNIGHT Kathleen Creighton

9907

Past secrets...
Deadly Deceptions...
The most intimate betrayal...
Dangerous
LIAISONS
3 full length stories in one volume
by Ann Major, Rebecca York
and Lindsay McKenna
On sale 18th June 1999
Available at most branches of WH Smith, Tesco, Asda,
Martins, Borders, Easons, Volume One/James Thin
and most good paperback bookshops

Sometimes bringing up baby can bring surprises —and showers of love! For the cutest and cuddliest heroes and heroines, choose the Special Edition™ book marked

That's my baby!

books and a surprise gift!

We would like to take this opportunity to thank you for reading this Silhouette® book by offering you the chance to take FOUR more specially selected titles from the Special Edition™ series absolutely FREE! We're also making this offer to introduce you to the benefits of the Reader Service™—

- ★ FREE home delivery
- ★ FREE gifts and competitions
- ★ FREE monthly Newsletter
- ★ Exclusive Reader Service discounts
- ★ Books available before they're in the shops

Accepting these FREE books and gift places you under no obligation to buy, you may cancel at any time, even after receiving your free shipment. Simply complete your details below and return the entire page to the address below. *You don't even need a stamp!*

YES! Please send me 4 free Special Edition books and a surprise gift. I understand that unless you hear from me, I will receive 6 superb new titles every month for just £2.70 each, postage and packing free. I am under no obligation to purchase any books and may cancel my subscription at any time. The free books and gift will be mine to keep in any case.

E9EA

Ms/Mrs/Miss/Mr ....Initials................................

BLOCK CAPITALS PLEASE

Surname ....

Address ....

....

....Postcode......................

Send this whole page to:
THE READER SERVICE, FREEPOST CN81, CROYDON, CR9 3WZ
(Eire readers please send coupon to: P.O. BOX 4546, DUBLIN 24.)